ARTEMIS

SPEED DATING WITH THE DENIZENS OF THE UNDERWORLD

BOOK THIRTY-FIVE

GINA KINCADE

NAUGHTY NIGHTS PRESS LLC• CANADA

ARTEMIS

Moonbeams and fated mates... what's a dragon shifter to do?

Artemis Chase has almost everything she ever wanted; she's the CEO of the Underworld's only bank and has a wonderful son. She's just missing the romance. Enter the perfect man, Lee. But she's never met him except through her son's stories.

Finley McKellen is happy his brothers found their mates, but he's lonely. He meets the perfect woman, except that she has a kid. Kids are messy, loud, and chaotic; not something he wants to deal with, especially since he's helping out

Maddie at her daycare during her last month of pregnancy.

When Alexander is kidnapped, it brings Artemis and Finley together, but will they be able to save the boy and their relationship, or is it doomed from the start?

Artemis is book thirty-five in the Speed Dating with the Denizens of the Underworld shared world, featuring a classy Moon Goddess, a protective dragon shifter, and more.

CHAPTER ONE

THE *CLICK-CLACK* OF Artemis Chase's four-inch spiked slingback heels echoed through the marble halls of Purgatory's only bank. The shuffle of sneakers followed, her assistant, Luna, right behind her.

"And Charon wants to open a branch on his flagship casino cruise ship. He's sent you a proposal."

"At least he knows how to do things

properly," Artemis said. "Put the report on my desk and I'll look at the numbers this afternoon."

"Yes, Miss Chase."

"Any word from the jackass?" Artemis felt her stomach flip just thinking about the man.

"No, I still haven't been able to reach Mister Blanca," Luna replied apologetically. "I'll keep trying. There's still a couple weeks until the party."

Artemis sighed and rubbed her temples, lifting the arms of her glasses with her motion. "It shouldn't be this difficult to invite a man to his own son's birthday party."

"To be perfectly honest—" Luna stopped abruptly.

"Go on." Artemis raised an eyebrow at

her assistant.

Luna swallowed hard and looked at a spot just above Artemis's left ear. "He hasn't even met your son. Why bother reaching out at all?"

"Valid question." Artemis continued on the way to the secondary meeting room. "Trust me, I don't do it for me. If it was just me, I would never contact that bastard again. But Alexander may want to know his father. Maybe he's happy now, but in the future..." Artemis paused in front of a mirrored wall, checking her appearance for any flaws.

"You have a wisp of hair coming out of your French braid," Luna said, shifting her clipboard onto one hip and reaching into the bag swinging at her side. "I've got it, hang on..." She pulled out a comb and a travel-sized bottle of hairspray before working her magic to get the midnight-black hair to lay flat again. "And you've half chewed off your lipstick." Luna handed her boss a wipe to remove the rest while she searched in her bag for the small tubes. "Pink, nude, or red?"

Artemis studied herself in the mirror. Today, she was wearing a pencil skirt suit, high-waisted with a flared jacket. Underneath the jacket was her favorite sheer white blouse with small red cherries scattered across it. "Red, if it matches the cherries."

Luna popped the cap of the tube of lipstick and offered it to her boss, who swiped it over the back of her hand. "Perfect match," Luna decided.

Quickly applying the lipstick, Artemis blotted her lips, checked her teeth, and cleaned off her hand. "All good?"

"Couldn't be better," Luna said.

"There's no way I could do this without you. The amount of care I have to take in my appearance when a man can show up to a meeting with their shirt untucked and tie undone..." Artemis seethed for a minute.

"Did you catch a glimpse of Mister Mercury when he arrived?" Luna asked, surprised.

"I didn't need to. I know his type." Artemis rolled her shoulders back and continued on her way to the meeting room.

"He seemed pretty pissed when I instructed security to bring him here rather than your office." Luna trotted along beside her. She checked her clipboard. "And you have a board meeting in thirty minutes."

Artemis paused, one elegantly manicured hand resting on the handle of the door to the meeting room. She took the file regarding Mercury from Luna and opened the door. "No, I have a board meeting in ten minutes."

Ignoring Luna's gasp as the door closed between them, Artemis tapped the file into the palm of one hand as she examined the man who had come to meet with her.

Mercury was dressed exactly as she had predicted, shirt one size too large, untucked, with his tie loose around his neck. He hadn't even bothered to bring a jacket, as far as she could see. His hair was slicked back with so much product that she could smell it from across the room, although perhaps that was his cologne.

The guy didn't stand up to greet her, which...

Come on. Rude!

She tossed the file on the table between them and it slid toward him.

He put his hand on it, but didn't open it. "I hear you might be expanding your business."

Artemis raised a perfect eyebrow. "I have a few proposals I'm looking at," she said, not wanting to commit to anything. She hadn't looked at Charon's paperwork yet, afterall.

How does Mercury know about that?

"Is that really a wise idea?" Mercury sneered. "Maybe you should stick to what you know." He opened the file to reveal a blank paper. "What is this?"

"Your reason for being here," Artemis quipped.

"There's nothing here."

"Precisely. Our meeting is done. Good day." She turned abruptly and left the room, leaving a spluttering Mercury behind.

Luna fell into step beside her. "You know, the last time someone talked to him like that, he sent them a deer's head in a box."

"I'm not afraid of him," Artemis scowled. "And if that's true, he should be *very* afraid of me."

"Yes, Miss Chase," Luna replied

meekly.

"Submissiveness doesn't suit you, Luna," Artemis said. At the boardroom, she straightened her jacket, took the offered file, and raised her chin. "Bet?"

"Twenty mansplains, only three correct."

"I'll take that." Artemis smiled. "Lunch on the loser?"

"ButterNut Bakery?"

"Where else?"

The meeting with the board members proceeded exactly as Luna predicted. The two women left the bank immediately following the closing remarks.

"Is there somewhere I can go to scream?" Artemis asked tightly. "I am so sick of being dismissed because of my gender!"

Luna nodded sympathetically. "Maybe you should join a gym or Odin's fight club, Valhalla's Throne, to blow off some steam."

That broke Artemis's bad mood. She burst into gales of laughter. "Can you imagine *me* in a fight club? I'd break a nail!" She got herself under control with difficulty. "No, I'll go to an extra pilates class. Do you think I can squeeze one in this afternoon?"

After consulting both Artemis's schedule and the local gym's classes, Luna said, "There's a class at two this afternoon that you can make if you can speed-read Charon's proposal beforehand."

"How many pages is it?"

"Three hundred."

Artemis gaped at her. "What?"

"Well, two hundred and ninety-eight, but I thought rounding up made more sense. It's single-sided, if that helps." Luna opened the door to ButterNut Bakery, and the tempting scents within washed over them.

"Not particularly." Artemis rubbed her temples as they got in line. "I need a break. No, scratch that, I need to get laid."

Luna chuckled. "That shouldn't be too difficult. I mean, look at you! You're gorgeous."

"Thank you for the compliment." Artemis sighed. "Unfortunately, guys look at me and are intimidated. It could be that I'm a Goddess, or maybe that I'm a CEO, or maybe just that I'm smart. Whatever it is, whenever I meet a guy, it doesn't usually end all that satisfactorily."

"Can I ask an impertinent question?" Luna asked hesitantly after she'd placed her order.

"You can get away with quite a bit. Go ahead." Artemis told Demi, the baker, her order, and paid for both lunches.

"How did you end up with Alexander's father?"

"He liked the feeling of power he got from being with me," Artemis said dryly. "Maybe I should amend my previous statement. It doesn't usually end satisfactorily for me *in bed*. The only good thing to come out of that relationship is Alexander."

"He's a darling," Luna agreed readily.

"Excuse me, I couldn't help but overhear," Hera, Demi's sister, said. "Artemis, you're looking for a guy?"

Artemis shrugged. "I'd settle for a good vibrator at this point."

Hera chuckled. "Tonight is Aphrodite and Eve's speed dating event for the month. Maybe you'll get lucky?"

"Speed dating?" Artemis said thoughtfully. Then she shook her head dismissively. "It sounds like fun, but there's no way I could get a babysitter on such short notice."

"I could do it," Luna volunteered.

"I run you ragged enough during the day," Artemis protested.

"Then pay me double the going rate." Luna grinned. "I don't mind. I haven't seen Alexander in weeks."

"I met my mate thanks to them," Hera continued. "He's such a gentleman." She lowered her voice conspiratorially. "And I'm always more than satisfied."

"I..." Artemis blinked. "I guess I don't have a good reason to say no. Can you give me the details for the event?"

"I'll write it all down for you and bring them with your food," Hera told her. "Go find a seat."

"This is so outside my expectations," Artemis said, sitting at a table in the corner.

"Then maybe it'll work!" Luna said.

"Maybe." It looked like some of Luna's optimism was rubbing off on her.

***

After a long afternoon, Artemis headed to the daycare to pick up Alexander.

"Mom!" Alexander cried the instant she walked in the front door.

Her heart swelled with love for him. He was such a darling. "Hello, sweetheart. Did you have a good day today?"

"Yes! We met Lee today!"

"Jaden's brother," Maddie, the owner of the daycare, explained. "He and Augustine are taking over duties when I have appointments and when the baby comes."

"Can I feel the baby move?" Alexander asked, his hands held tightly behind his back.

"I'm sorry sweetie, she's not moving right now because I've been walking around. The movement puts her to sleep." Maddie put her hand on her belly. "But you can feel her back if you'd like."

"Yes!"

Maddie took his hand and placed it where hers had been. "Press gently," she instructed. "You can rub her back... Yes, just like that. Do you feel her?"

Alexander's eyes were wide. "I can!" He beamed up at Maddie. "Thank you!" He took Artemis's hand. "Mom, how did the baby get in there? I asked Maddie, but she said I had to ask you. Doesn't she know?"

Artemis chuckled. "Of course she knows, sweetheart. She wanted to make sure that I was okay with you knowing. The baby grew inside her, like a plant grows in the ground."

Alexander considered that silently. Artemis knew he'd have more questions for her in a few minutes.

"See you tomorrow," Maddie said.

"Bye." Mother and son left the building, driving the short distance to home.

"Who put the baby inside her?" Alexander asked.

"Jaden and Maddie did," Artemis replied.

"Did I grow inside you?"

"Yes, you did."

"Could you feel my back through your skin?"

Artemis chuckled. "Yes. I also saw your foot once. You were a very strong baby. You even broke one of my ribs once."

"I'm sorry, Mom." Alexander's bottom lip quivered.

"You didn't do it on purpose and I don't blame you, but thank you for the apology." Artemis smiled at him in the rearview mirror. "Did you have any more questions about the baby?"

"Not right now," Alexander replied.

"You can ask me at any time." They turned onto their street. "How would you like Luna to look after you tonight?"

"Luna!" Alexander wiggled in his seat. "Yes! She tells great bedtime stories about a princess on the moon!"

"That sounds amazing! You should draw me some of the scenes at Maddie's some time."

Alexander stared at her. "Yes!" he

squeaked. "I want to do that!"

Artemis laughed. "I'm glad you like the suggestion. What would you like for dinner tonight, chicken salad or fish taco bowl?"

"Fish! Can I help?"

"Definitely. What's the first thing we need to do?"

"Turn on the oven!"

"No, that's second."

Alexander thought about it and Artemis waited patiently while she unlocked the front door of their house.

"Wash our hands," he finally replied.

"Excellent."

Artemis loved cooking with her son. He was so enthusiastic about flavors and trying new recipes. She gave him the job of cutting vegetables using the food processor, keeping a close eye on him to make sure he kept his fingers out of the way of the blade inside the machine.

They fed Elati, her fawn, while the fish cooked, and then ate their own dinner on the back porch, surrounded by the garden. Most of the flowers weren't open yet, but would bloom in the moonlight. Tomorrow would be the full moon, and Artemis looked forward to bathing in the pool in her backyard, replenishing her Goddess strength.

She didn't exactly *need* it, but it helped her keep her temper at work. It was like a boost of caffeine after a week of crappy sleep.

"Lee learned how to change diapers today. I helped him change Lyta's diaper. He didn't know where the tabs were."

Alexander giggled. "I was a big help."

"I'm not surprised to hear that. You're a big help to me too." Artemis cleared her plate and their glasses, while Alexander carried his plate behind her. "I've got about an hour before Luna gets here. What would you like to do?"

"Can we do yoga?" Alexander asked, cocking his head to one side.

"Sure kiddo. Monkey yoga, or side by side?"

"Monkey."

"*You're* a monkey," Artemis teased.

"No, I'm not." Alexander pouted.

"What are you then?"

"I'm Alexander."

"Alexander the monkey."

He thought about that. "Okay."

Monkey yoga involved Alexander

clinging to her while she moved slowly through various poses. Artemis had started doing it when he'd been too small to hold on, wearing him in a sling. Once he'd had enough grip strength, he alternated hugging her from behind or the front, depending on the pose. They both loved the bonding the exercise gave them.

"Want to help me choose what to wear tonight?" Artemis asked after she had run through the usual routine.

"Where are you going?"

"I'm going to a party to meet some new friends."

"Will I get to meet them?"

"Only if I really like the person," Artemis said.

"Okay." Alexander followed her to her

room. "You should wear the flower shirt."

"Why?" Artemis stripped out of her workout clothes behind a screen and put on a robe.

"Because I like it."

Artemis smiled. "That's a great reason. What should I wear on the bottom half of me?"

"A swishy skirt. But you have to spin for me," Alexander said seriously.

"I can do that. And shoes?"

"Can I play with them?"

"Only if you're really careful." Artemis headed for the bathroom off her bedroom. "Stay in my room, please. I'm going to take a quick shower."

"Okay, Mom."

When she got out of the shower, she

saw that Alexander had chosen a pair of bright purple platform shoes with a peep toe. The rest of her shoes were in piles on the floor. "Are you going to clean all of this up?"

"Can you help?" Alexander said in a small voice. "It's a lot."

"It is, isn't it? What could you have done differently, so that it didn't get to be such a mess?"

"Only two shoes at a time?"

"That probably would have helped." Artemis bit the inside of her cheek to stop her laughter.

"Yeah."

CHAPTER TWO

"WHAT DO YOU mean, it's my turn?" Finley asked.

"I visited the daycare yesterday," Augustine replied. "Maddie would like to show you the ropes as well."

"It has to be today?" Finley asked. He'd been hoping to get in an extra long workout, since he didn't have a shift at Valhalla's Throne today.

"She has a doctor's appointment

tomorrow afternoon, and I am at the Valhalla's." Augustine shrugged apologetically. "You are the best choice."

"Am I?" Finley muttered under his breath. "Okay, I'll head over after lunch."

"It would be better if you went now," Augustine said. "The routine is very specific."

"Hestia will be taking the lead though, right?" Finley asked anxiously. "I won't have to remember everything on my own?"

"Of course she will." Augustine patted Finley's shoulder. "You will be fine, little brother."

"Jaden owes me big for this," Finley muttered, heading back up the stairs to get dressed to deal with small children.

When he arrived at the daycare, he

could hear the children shouting in the big backyard.

How many did Jaden say Maddie looked after? This sounds like twenty!

Feeling nervous, Finley rang the doorbell, hoping that it could be heard over the ruckus.

Fortunately, it seemed like it could, as Maddie greeted him not long after. "Come in and meet the kids!" she said, beaming. "We're out back for another five or so minutes. I'm teaching the boys how to do a cartwheel."

Finley raised an eyebrow and looked down at her belly. "At eight months pregnant?"

"I'm not doing the cartwheels, they are." Maddie rubbed one hand protectively over her stomach. "This would throw off my balance for sure!"

"Exactly what I was thinking." Finley scratched at his stubble. "I could teach them how to do a headstand."

"They would love that."

The backyard was half grass, a quarter sand, and a quarter playground. The boys were tumbling on the grass while the girls were playing in the sand.

"Don't eat that, Lyta," Maddie said, and the little girl pouted as she took the shovel out of her mouth. "We'll be eating lunch soon. Are your teeth bothering you?"

"Ah!" Lyta said, pushing herself up onto her feet and walking unsteadily toward Maddie.

"Are your hands clean?" Maddie asked Finley.

"I touched my doorknob and your doorbell after washing my face this morning," Finley replied.

"Excellent. Just rub your finger along her gums. Her molars are bothering her, poor thing."

Next thing Finley knew, he had an armful of toddler. "Umm, hi," he said to the girl.

"Hi," she repeated, staring at him with large brown eyes.

"I hear your teeth are coming in?" He felt silly talking to the toddler like she knew what he was saying, but he didn't know how else to talk to her.

Lyta stuck a sandy finger in her mouth.

"Oh, ew," Finley said, making a face. "Sand isn't good for your tummy." He sucked in a deep breath.

I can't believe I'm doing this.

"Here, let me feel those gums."

Lyta grabbed his hand with both of hers and bit down, hard.

Finley swallowed a yelp and shifted the skin on his finger into dragon scales.

Lyta chirped and pulled his hand out, examining it intently.

"It's blue because I'm a blue dragon shifter," Finley explained. "Your bite hurt me, and this protects me."

Blinking her big brown eyes, Lyta seemed to consider his explanation seriously before sticking his finger back in her mouth.

"You're really good with her," Maddie said, returning to his side and rubbing one hand over the little girl's head.

"Apparently, the trick is to know when to protect myself," Finley said with a chuckle. "It's a good thing I'm a quick healer."

Maddie winced. "Sorry." She took Lyta from him. "Why don't you try teaching some headstands now? Alexander is the youngest, with blond hair, and Damien is the oldest, with black hair."

"Alexander," Finley repeated. "Damien."

"You've got this big guy," Maddie cheered him on.

Finley headed over to the two little boys. He'd never felt so tall as he did today. They didn't even come up to his waist. "Hey," he said once he was close enough to be heard. "Looks like you're having fun. Can you teach me how to do a cartwheel?"

"Yes!" Damien exclaimed.

"Start with one leg out," Alexander said. "And hands up!" He demonstrated.

Solemnly, Finley followed suit.

"And then you put your hands on the grass one at a time, jumping a bit," Damien continued. He bent and put his hands on the ground and hopped, his legs getting barely off the ground. He stood up, beaming.

Alexander fared no better, and Finley had to bite back a smile. He nodded and copied the boys exactly. "Like that?" he asked.

"Noooo," said Alexander slowly, frowning. "That's not what Maddie's looked like. Her legs went straight up in the air."

"Hmm," said Finley, pretending to concentrate hard. "Like this?" He did a handstand. "Now what?" he said, still upside down. "I think I'm stuck like this!"

"Lift a hand!" Damien suggested. "You'll fall down."

Finley shifted his weight onto one arm and lifted the other. "I'm still stuck!"

"Put your feet down!" Alexander said.

"Oh, that's better," Finley said after putting his feet down and collapsing in an exaggerated manner onto the grass. "I'm Finley. I'll be looking after you when Maddie's busy."

"Hestia too?" Alexander asked.

"Hestia will still be here, no worries."

"Gus too?"

It took Finley a moment to realize that Alexander meant Augustine. "Yes, Augustine and I will be taking turns. He's my brother, did you know that?"

"I have a big sister," Damien volunteered.

"You don't look like Gus."

"Well, no, we don't have the same birth parents," Finley admitted.

"Then how is he your brother?" Alexander asked.

"Do you know how adoption works?" When both boys shook their heads, Finley continued, "It's when you become a family with someone who isn't your parent by birth. My brothers and I became a family."

"You have more than one brother?" Damien asked.

"Jaden is my other brother. Have you met him?"

"Maddie's Jaden?" Alexander's gray eyes grew wide.

"That's right."

"Can you teach me to stand on my hands?" Damien asked, changing the subject abruptly.

Finley gasped dramatically. "You don't want to get stuck like that the way I did!"

"Yes, I do!" Damien shouted excitedly.

"Well, all right then. But we're going to start with headstands. They're more stable."

"Why?" Alexander asked.

Finley thought about how to explain it. "Have you built a tower with blocks?"

"Yes!"

"Have you noticed that when you make it skinny, it's more likely to fall down? And if you make a big base, it stays up better?" At their eager nods, Finley smiled. "A headstand is like a tower with a big base. You use your hands to make your base, the part that touches the ground, bigger. Does that make sense?"

Teaching the little boys headstands was easier said than done. They didn't seem to grasp the concept of *not wiggling*, for one, so they couldn't manage to stay up for even a second.

"Time for lunch!" Hestia called. "Everyone wash your hands, and then I need helpers to set the table!"

Finley was impressed by how well the two women worked together to organize the children. First, they brushed sand from their clothes at the doorway, and then helped the girls wash their hands. The boys only needed to be supervised, which Finley willingly stepped in to help with.

The boys scampered off to the kitchen, where they took out forks, spoons, plates, and cups to put on the table and counter.

Maddie cajoled the girls into their high chairs, giving them a handful of cheerios to occupy them while their lunch was organized, and they were joined by the boys, who played a boisterous game of "I Spy" while they waited.

"You do this every day?" Finley asked Maddie quietly. "I'm exhausted and I've only been here for half an hour!"

Maddie chuckled. "You get used to it." She shrugged. "It's not for everyone."

"I've got a whole new appreciation for you," Finley said.

"That's sweet. Here." She handed him two bowls of mac and cheese with chopped zucchini and chicken. "Try to get the girls to use their spoons, if you can."

"I'll try," Finley said with hesitation.

The attempt went about what he expected in some ways, and so much worse in others. He'd never seen a child get cheese sauce in their hair. Or discovered how difficult it was to take out.

Hestia took Atlanta into the bathroom after the meal to give her a quick bath while Maddie took care of the dishes.

Finley settled the boys with art supplies at the table and sat with Lyta with stacking blocks.

After a few minutes, the stench of ammonia hit Finley's sensitive nostrils. He raised an eyebrow at Lyta. "That's you, isn't it?"

Lyta shifted, obviously uncomfortable in her wet diaper.

"Maddie?" Finley called into the kitchen. "Lyta needs a diaper change!"

"That's fine. You can take care of it," Maddie replied.

Finley looked back down at the toddler. "Umm..."

"You have to learn sometime. Hestia won't be available all the time," Maddie teased.

"I can help you, Mister Lee."

Alexander was standing beside him, gray eyes serious in his small face.

"You know how to change a diaper?"

"Of course," he replied, with all the airs of an almost three-year-old.

"Alrighty then," Finley said, internally cringing and mentally promising himself to never use that phrase again.

Alexander led him over to the change table, and Finley put the toddler on top of it.

"Now what?"

"You open the snaps and take off the diaper. Here's a clean one and the wipes," Alexander said.

"How do you know so much about this?" Finley asked. "How old are you?"

"Almost three. Mom says I'm helpful."

"I bet she does."

"I like helping."

Finley smiled. He couldn't believe that he was finding something to smile about with these kids. "I'm glad you do. I would be completely lost without you."

"You're at Maddie's," Alexander said, frowning in confusion. "Did you forget?"

"Thank you, Alexander," Finley replied, stifling his laughter.

"You're welcome!" Alexander chirped before skipping back to Damien, who was painting on the wall.

Finley picked Lyta up. "Feel better?" he asked her.

"You may not feel comfortable with kids yet, but I think that will come with time," Maddie said, waddling up to him. "By the time this baby's out of me, you'll be able to take care of these kids with one hand tied behind your back."

"Not a chance," Finley replied with a shudder. He nodded at the freshly painted landscape on her wall. "Why are you letting him do that?"

"He's expressing himself creatively," Maddie said with a chuckle.

"But..." Finley trailed off.

"What, should I yell at him?" Maddie asked impishly. "He's not hurting anyone, is he?"

"No, of course not." Finley squirmed internally.

Maddie patted his shoulder. "You're a little tense. Maybe you should work out after this."

"Seriously," he muttered.

"Damien, sweetie," Maddie said,

walking over to the boy. "You remember that if you paint on paper, it will last longer, right? The wall has to be cleaned."

Damien pouted at her. "But I like this!"

"I do too," Maddie reassured him. "How about I leave it up while you copy it down on paper, and then you can help me wash the wall before we hang your picture on it. Would you like it in the same place?"

"Yeah! And then, maybe I can bring it home and hang it on my wall!" Damien said excitedly.

"That's a great idea! Would you like your paper flat on the table or pinned to an easel like a professional artist?"

"What's po-fish-al?" Damien asked.

"Mom's a po-fish-al," Alexander added to the conversation.

"She is!" Maddie agreed with a smile. "It's someone who does something for money. In this case, we're talking about an artist who paints for money."

"Your mom's a painter?" Damien asked.

Alexander shook his head. "No. She works in a bank."

"Yes, she does." Maddie focussed on Damien again. "Flat or easel?"

"Easel," Damien said after much consideration.

"Excellent choice. I'll even make you a palette out of a lid, would you like that?"

"Can I have one too?" Alexander asked, bouncing a bit.

Maddie raised an eyebrow.

"Please?" Alexander added angelically.

"Thank you," Maddie said.

Finley shook his head at her patience and calm demeanor. That situation would have gone quite differently if he'd been the only adult in charge. He had a lot to learn about taking messes in stride.

***

Later, as he was working out in the gym at Valhalla's Throne, he overheard two guys talking about a speed dating event one guy had attended the previous month.

"All sorts of women show up. Whatever you're into, you'll find someone who'll jump at you."

"No shit? Even if I'm not looking for something serious?"

"I'm not pulling your leg. I found a woman who just wanted a roll in the sack last month. The next one is tonight. You should totally check it out."

Finley's ears perked up and he carefully lowered the back press. "Is that Aphrodite and Eve's event?" he asked the two guys. Both other men were in a lower weight class than he was, so he wasn't sure of their names.

"You've heard of it?"

"Both of my brothers found their mates thanks to that thing. You're saying that not everyone who goes there wants a relationship?"

One guy shrugged. "Maybe if they don't find 'the one', they're happy with a

'Mister right now'. All I can say is that the girl I pulled had no complaints after the night with me."

"Right on!" They fist bumped.

Finley shook his head with a chuckle. "It's happening tonight, you said? Same place?"

"You thinking about checking it out?"

"I might. Been feeling a little restless lately, you know?"

"Hope you find someone to scratch that itch for you," one guy said with a laugh and an elbow nudge to the other's ribs.

"I think I'll head out," Finley said, bending to pick up his water bottle. "See you."

"It starts at eight!"

Finley waved a hand in

acknowledgement and headed for the brothers' private room to change before heading home for a proper shower. The one at work was horrible; cold beyond belief.

After showering and changing into a dark blue dress shirt and jeans without holes in them, he scrawled a note to Augustine on the fridge whiteboard.

Going out for the evening. Will be on time for Maddie's in the am.

The weather was warm when he stepped out the door and he almost regretted wearing long sleeves. A quick glance at his watch told him he didn't have time to change. "I'll manage," he muttered as he rolled up his sleeves. "Don't want to be late to meet my destiny," he joked.

CHAPTER THREE

ARTEMIS ASSESSED THE men in the bar at the speed dating event over the rim of her wine glass. Several looked promising, making her heart speed up in anticipation. Hopefully one of them would be as attracted to her.

She was already sitting at a table, not really wanting to mingle before the event took place. In the past, the longer people talked to her, the less they wanted to stick around. A five minute speed date was the perfect pace for her.

She hoped.

She took another sip of the sweet red, the fruity flavors bursting across her taste buds. Artemis put the glass down on the table, not wanting to drink it too quickly. She wanted a buzz, not to get drunk. Switching which ankle was crossed in front, she shifted on her chair.

When is this going to start?

Finally, the stunningly beautiful Aphrodite appeared at the front of the room and got their attention. "Good evening, everyone! If you wouldn't mind taking your seats..."

There was a flurry of activity as people hurried to follow the directions.

"Excellent. Your dates will be five minutes each. Once you have changed tables, you will have ten seconds to mark down your impressions of your previous date before the next one starts. Any questions before we begin?" Aphrodite paused. "Your first date starts now."

Artemis smiled at the dark-skinned man sitting across from her. She took in his brown eyes and elegantly-trimmed goatee.

He's extremely attractive.

"Artemis," she introduced herself.

"My name is Abdullah," he replied in a thick accent, holding out his hand to her. "It is my pleasure to make your acquaintance. What is it that you do?"

"Oh, I'm in finance," Artemis said

flippantly. His voice was making it difficult for her to think. "And you?"

"I am the head chef of a restaurant," he said.

"Really? What type of food?" Artemis leaned forward eagerly.

"Middle-Eastern." He smiled. "Have you ever tried it?"

"Oh yes. I hand-make samosas with my son for dinner once a month."

"Oh, you have a son." Abdullah pulled back slightly.

Artemis's heart sank. "Yes, he's almost three. We do a lot together. But I don't want to introduce him to anyone for a while."

"Hmm, yes, I quite agree," he said noncommittally.

She sighed.

One date down, thirteen to go.

Every time a new date started, Artemis made a mental note not to mention Alexander, but it always slipped out, and the men responded the same way each time; complete disinterest.

Artemis sipped the last of her wine between dates, and considered getting another glass. It was almost the end of the event, and nobody seemed interested. She wasn't sure what she'd come here for, a fling or something more, but it was looking more and more like she'd leave empty handed tonight. Frustrated with herself, she looked up at her last date of the evening.

Up and up, gaze trailing over hard muscle, broad shoulders, and twinkly blue eyes. "Hi," she said a little breathlessly.

"Hi." He smiled at her. "How has your evening been?"

She waved a dismissive hand. "Better now."

His smile widened. "I'm Finley."

"Artemis." She couldn't stop staring at his forearms, framed by rolled up dark blue sleeves. "You are a very attractive man."

Finley chuckled. "Thank you. You're stunningly beautiful yourself. Can I guess your occupation before you guess mine?"

"Challenge accepted." She liked this. "You first?"

"I laid down the terms. You get the first guess."

"All right." She bit her lip, evaluating

him. "Construction."

"Nice. I do know my way around a power tool or two, but no." Finley crossed his arms. "Your posture is perfect, so I'm thinking something where you're the boss."

"Is that your guess?"

"If I'm right, it narrows the search."

"You are right. So far." Artemis noticed the calluses on his fingers. "A musician?"

Finley chuckled. "I can sing, but most people complain when they hear it. No. A job where you're in charge. The CEO of a company?"

Artemis winced internally.

Was she that obvious?

Would he find that too much?

"Yes. You're very good at this. Are you

in security?”

“No. Is CEO not enough? I need to guess which company?”

“I like to win, and the harder your job is, the more likely I am to win,” Artemis said playfully.

“You know, I’ve played this game with all the other ladies here, and none of them have asked me to identify their place of work,” Finley said, raising an eyebrow. “How about we up the stakes a little? If one of us guesses the place of work of the other, the winner gets a favor.”

“I like that.”

“CEO of a manufacturing company.”

“No. Are you a wrestler?”

Finley hummed slightly. “Yes, I guess that could describe what I do. Are you the CEO of a distribution company?"

"No. Do you work at Valhalla's Throne?"

Finley's jaw dropped. "How do you know about that place?"

"It's a secret that everyone knows about," Artemis replied. "Am I right?"

"Yeah, you are," he admitted. "I'm impressed."

"So am I." She raked her gaze over his form again. "From what I've heard of that place, you should look much more bruised than you are. You must either be really good or heal really fast."

"Both." He grinned at her. "Are you going to tell me where you work?"

"Maybe on the next date," she teased.

"Confident, aren't you?"

"Am I right?" she asked again.

Artemis felt his gaze burn over her as he took his time to answer her.

"You are definitely the most interesting woman I've met this evening. I admit I came here for a quick pick-up, but now..." Finley let his sentence hang in the air between them.

"Would you think less of me if I said I was thinking along the same lines?" Artemis asked boldly.

"Not at all." He opened his mouth to say more, but was interrupted by Aphrodite speaking.

"We will collect your papers and put you in touch with your matches before the end of the evening. If you would please make your way to Eve..."

Artemis put her hand on one of Finley's forearms. The dusting of hair tickled her palm and the warmth from his skin was electric, as was the intensity of his eyes when he looked at her. "I already know that I'm not a match with any of the others. And I'm ready to use my favor."

Finley grinned. "Are you? They were too intimidated by a woman CEO?"

"Something like that." Artemis didn't really want to bring up Alexander.

What if Finley has the same reaction?

"I want you to bring me to the bathroom and get me off."

"You really are the most interesting woman," Finley said with a laugh. "It would be my pleasure, my lady." He climbed to his feet and offered his hand to her.

Artemis took it, marveling at their

size difference. He practically loomed over her. What he'd feel like moving over her, inside her... She shook her head. There was no reason to dwell on what would probably never happen.

Nervous laughter was bubbling up inside her by the time they reached the bathrooms. Finley let her choose which one to go in. She picked the men's. Men were less likely to need it, she reasoned.

The instant the door closed behind them, Finley drew her close, one large hand cupping the back of her head. His eyes searched hers. "Do you still want this?"

"One hundred percent," she said firmly. "Kiss me."

Drawing out the anticipation, Finley lowered his head slowly. Artemis wrapped her arms around his neck, hoping that would encourage him to speed up, but she couldn't move him. He paused a hair's breadth away from her lips, his breath fanning over her face and smelling like peppermint.

She closed her eyes, suddenly anxious about what her breath might smell like, but all thoughts fled when his lips brushed hers.

The kiss began with a cautious press of lips, but quickly escalated to tongues dancing, breathing hot into each other's mouths. All Artemis knew was that she needed to be closer to this man; she needed to be surrounded by him. She hiked one leg up his thigh, and he grabbed it under her knee, lifting her with ease and pressing her against the wall, a low rumble of a growl echoing through his chest.

Artemis had never felt so desired. She tipped her head back to rest against the wall as he nipped and sucked down her neck.

"You taste so sweet," he rasped. "Want to lick you everywhere."

"Yes!" she moaned in approval as he reached her clavicle.

He must have taken that as permission, hiking her body higher up the wall as his lips continued their passage down the low cut v-neck of her floral shirt. Artemis pulled on the sleeves, making the material sag over her breasts.

"Can I?" Finley asked, nuzzling her sternum.

"Please," she begged.

Using his teeth, he tugged the material out of the way, exposing her breasts to the warm air. "Beautiful," he said, taking her in. "I like the jewelry."

Artemis blushed. She'd gotten barbell piercings in her nipples after she'd finished nursing Alexander a couple years ago, but nobody had ever seen them before. "They feel good when I'm turned on," she confided.

"Yeah?" Finley's eyes lightened to an icy blue, almost completely swallowed by the dark pupil. "How do they feel now?"

"*Really* good," she whispered.

He bent and took one into his mouth, tongue flicking over the metal and sending zings of pleasure straight to her clit. Releasing it with a pop, a string of saliva still connecting his mouth to her breast, he looked up at her. "And now?"

"Fucking fantastic," she moaned.

He suckled the other side into his mouth, paying it the same attention as he had the first, drawing them both into stiff rosy peaks. "You are full of surprises," he murmured, pulling away again. "I'm going to eat you out now."

"You are?" Artemis squeaked. She'd expected him to finger her, not this.

"Is that okay?" he asked.

"Nobody has ever..." she trailed off, embarrassed.

Finley wasn't laughing at her. "If you don't want me to, I won't. But I would really enjoy it."

He left the decision up to her. Artemis chewed on her lip as she thought about it. "If I don't like it…"

"I'll stop immediately," he promised.

"How are you going to—oh!" Artemis exclaimed as he lifted her up even higher, hooking her legs over his shoulders.

This freed up his hands, which he ran up her calves. "These are pretty, but they'll make it difficult to get at you."

"No, they won't." Artemis lifted her skirt, revealing the garter belt holding up the thigh-high stockings. Underneath, she wore a purple thong that matched her heels.

"Daaamn," Finley drawled. "You're so sexy. Hold your skirt for me. I want to see what I'm doing." His hands continued up her legs, tracing the straps of the garter, until they reached the apex of her thighs. "You've soaked through your panties. Is that because of me?"

"*Finley,*" she gasped as he traced her through the purple cotton. "Stop teasing."

"I'm thoroughly enjoying this," Finley replied, eyes twinkling with mischief. He turned his head and pressed a kiss on her thigh. "Watching you squirm is my new favorite obsession." One finger pulled the wet material to the side, exposing her to his hungry gaze. "You smell amazing."

Artemis actually did squirm then, hesitant about this new experience. When would he— "Oh my God!" she whimpered as he shifted forward, lifting her legs so that they draped further down his back and pinning her hips against the wall.

He explored her lower lips as expertly as he had kissed her earlier, hungrily lapping up her juices before they dripped down his chin. She felt a finger at her entrance, circling lightly, and moaned an eager "Yes!" before he speared into her, his thick finger filling and stretching her. Her hips rocked slightly, not having much space but needing to move against the pleasure that Finley was giving her.

"Ohhhhhh," she groaned when he applied suction to her clit, flicking across it with his tongue.

Artemis arched her back, the top of her head brushing against the ceiling, and gripped Finley's hair with one hand, her fingers threading through his close-cropped curls to his scalp. *"Finley,"* she squeaked. "I'm close!"

A low rumble from deep within his chest echoed through the empty bathroom as his tongue picked up speed.

"Fuck!" Artemis muttered to herself mindlessly, riding his face with shuddering hips. "Almo—ohhh *God!*" Her orgasm caught her by surprise, exploding with a force that was unexpected in its intensity. Artemis actually saw sparks behind her closed eyelids. She didn't know that could happen.

Coming down slowly, she relaxed her grip on Finley's hair and belatedly realized that she'd been squeezing his head between her thighs.

"Sorry," she apologized.

"Don't you *dare*," Finley said, blinking up at her. "That was incredible." He sucked his finger into his mouth and hummed, eyes rolling back. "Delicious."

"I have no comparison, but you are *really* good at that," Artemis said.

Finley shrugged. "When you enjoy something, you do it well." He smirked cheekily at her as he lowered her down the wall. "You're glowing."

Artemis blinked, confused. "Um... Thank you?"

"No, I mean literally." He led her over to the sinks and the mirrors behind them.

Sure enough, she was emitting a white light from her skin. "That's new," she said.

"It's beautiful. Reminds me of the

moon," Finley reassured her.

Chuckling, Artemis looked up at him.

Damn, he's tall. "I *am* the Goddess of the moon." Her small hand trailed down his hard abdomen to his belt. "Want me to take care of this for you?"

He took her hand in his. "I think we've occupied this bathroom long enough. Some other time?"

"I look forward to it." Artemis closed her eyes and sucked in a couple deep breaths, hoping to dim her glow a little. Peeking at herself in the mirror, she saw it was only a little effective.

"So, the Moon Goddess, huh?" Finley said, leaning against the wall next to the sinks, pinning her with his gaze.

"Yes." Artemis adjusted her shirt and underwear, trying to ignore Finley's knowing grin. "Goddesses are just as deserving as everyone else to date, don't you think?"

"Oh yes. Completely," Finley agreed readily. "That shirt looks amazing on you, by the way."

"Thank you. My son told me I should wear it tonight."

"Your son?"

Oh no.

"Yes. Don't worry, the father isn't in the picture."

"I'm sorry you don't have the support you need to raise your child."

"We do all right," she said stiffly, pushing her glasses up her nose. Her glow was completely gone now.

Finley checked his watch as they left the bathroom. "Would you look at the time? I promised my brother I'd be home by now. I'll talk to you later, okay?"

"Okay," she said, and then he was gone before she could even give him her number. She could practically see the cartoon smoke trails in his wake.

Well, fuck.

CHAPTER FOUR

FINLEY GROANED AS he rolled out of bed the next morning.

Far too early to be up. Far too early to deal with children.

"I love my brother," he grumbled, stretching one arm and then the other over his head. "He owes me."

He moved through his kung fu forms smoothly, the repetitive motions soothing his mind. By the time he'd finished, he felt awake and more like himself. He tossed on clothing and trotted downstairs for breakfast.

Jaden was in the kitchen. "Thought you might want an omelet."

Finley raised an eyebrow. "This doesn't count as payment."

"Of course not!" Jaden affected a shocked expression.

"If I hadn't brought it up, you might have tried."

"Hey, I'm having a kid. I've moved past those infantile tricks," Jaden said haughtily.

"I'll believe that when I see it." Finley pulled up a chair at the kitchen island. "Mushrooms, cheddar, bacon, and chives, please."

"Coming right up. In a wrap,

sandwich, or as is?" Jaden expertly cracked three eggs into a bowl and scooped large handfuls of toppings into a pan. He shuffled the pan with a practiced twist of his wrist before pouring cream into the eggs and picking up a whisk.

"Since you seem to be doing them the fancy way, I'll take it as is. Since when did you learn how to cook like this?" Finley asked admiringly.

"When do you think?" Jaden replied, adding salt and beating the egg-cream mixture. "Maddie has been craving eggs practically nonstop."

"Whipped looks good on you, little bro," Finley teased, and then bit his tongue. "Sorry. That's not what I—"

"I know what you meant." Jaden

flipped the toppings again and poured them into a separate bowl, emptying the egg mixture into the pan.

Finley stayed quiet, thinking about how panicked he'd felt when Jaden had been kidnapped and beaten within an inch of his life not even a year before. His kidnappers, led by an ancient diamond dragon shifter, had wanted him to win—and lose—matches for them, so that their gambling ring would make more money.

When they started fighting at Valhalla's Throne the brothers had agreed upon a system, once they realized that nobody could beat them in their respective weight classes, whereupon they would roll a dice before starting work, and based on that roll, they would win or throw the match.

Jaden had added the toppings to the egg and folded them in once by the time Finley found his voice again. "I'm glad Maddie's taught you some skills in the kitchen that go beyond making cereal."

Snorting his amusement, Jaden folded the omelet once more. "We all know that Auggie's the real cook in this family. How are you going to fend for yourself once he moves in with his mate?"

"You know damn well that her name is Hera," Finley said. "And I'll alternate meals at your houses, obviously."

"Right, because that's sustainable." Jaden shook his head and lifted the omelet onto a plate, which he sent spinning over the countertop to Finley.

"Maybe you should try looking for a mate of your own?"

"I think I'd be better off hiring a chef than finding a woman just because I can't cook," Finley said wryly. "Or even better, maybe I'll take some cooking classes."

Jaden snickered. "I bet you'd look cute in an apron."

"If you can rock one, so can I," Finley retorted.

"Thanks for the compliment." Jaden preened, batting his eyelashes.

Finley ignored him and focused on his plate, cutting a bite off the edge of the egg. "The way you're waiting around makes me wonder if you poisoned this. Or are you just that insecure about your cooking abilities?"

"Shut up and eat it," Jaden growled.

"Hold your dragon." Finley took the bite off his fork and chewed it thoughtfully, rolling the flavors around on his tongue before swallowing. Silently, with a straight face, he cut a new bite from the omelet and ate it.

Finally, Jaden couldn't take it any longer. "Well?" he practically exploded.

"It's edible," Finley replied.

Jaden threw his hands in the air and stalked out of the kitchen.

Finley laughed. "Come back! It's delicious. Really."

"You are the *worst* brother," Jaden grumbled as he returned.

"Does the worst brother look after children all day for your mate when he despises the messy little creatures?"

Finley asked, before eating another bite.

"Those kids are adorable and you know it."

Finley winced. "One of them was painting *on the wall* yesterday!"

"So? It's not your house. Whatever they do, Maddie and Hestia will take care of it. You just have to keep them occupied, entertained, and safe," Jaden pointed out.

"I have no idea what to do with kids that small," Finley whined. "I can't teach them martial arts; they're too young for the discipline needed."

"I would argue that some adults don't have the discipline for martial arts," Jaden muttered under his breath. "That doesn't matter. Hestia will lead the activities. You're an extra pair of hands."

"That makes me feel so welcomed."

"It should." Jaden started washing the dishes and cleaning the counter around the stovetop. "Where were you last night? Auggie said you weren't going to be home until late."

"Oh, I tried out that speed dating thing. Heard some guys at Valhalla's mention it was a good place to pick up." Finley nodded at him. "You two had some luck there as well."

Jaden rolled his eyes. "Maddie was the best one there. How'd you make out?"

Finley thought about the gorgeous Goddess he'd tasted the night before, how pliant she'd been in his arms, how his body craved her even now. "There was one woman, but she's a single mom.”

“So? I thought you only wanted to pick up?”

“She seemed interested in more than that.” Finley shrugged and shifted on his chair, mentally telling his cock to stand down. “I’m not even sure I can handle a relationship with a woman, let alone with a child as well.”

“Your call, bro.” Jaden gave the counter a swipe with the drying cloth and checked his watch. “We’d better go. Maddie’s appointment is in half an hour.”

“Why isn’t Hera looking after Maddie?” Finley asked as they headed for the daycare.

“She is, but Maddie’s pregnancy is considered high risk.” Jaden frowned.

"Something about her pelvis being too narrow. Hera wants her to be checked out at the hospital and to meet the team that'll be on hand when the time comes for the delivery. While we're there today, the doctors want to do some routine checkups and ultrasounds."

"Sounds a little scary," Finley said.

"Hera said that it's better to be safe than sorry. I'm inclined to agree with her. I want Maddie to be as safe as possible."

"Me too. Sounds like she's in good hands." The daycare was visible now and Finley felt his anxiety rise, the contents of his stomach flip-flopping around.

Why did I agree to this?

Maddie's beaming smile when she met them at the door reminded him.

Right, because it's hard to say no to her.

"Come on in!" she said, opening the door fully. "Lyta and Atlanta are still sleeping and Hestia is reading to Alexander and Damien. Do you remember who everyone is?"

"I've got it, thanks," Finley replied anxiously.

"Hestia is in charge, so just do what she says and you'll be fine." Maddie patted his arm. "I should be back near the end of the pick-ups to help clean up. See you then." She took Jaden's arm and they left.

Finley wandered into the large playroom and sat on one of the big couches to listen to the story Hestia was reading. It was about how a prince and a farm boy met and fell in love. The art was pretty, he could see from his position, and the boys were entranced by the story.

A piercing cry cut the story short and Hestia moved to put the book away, but Finley got to his feet. "Keep reading, I'll get her."

"Holler if you need help," Hestia replied with a smile. "That sounded like Atlanta, but she'll wake Lyta in— Oh, yeah, there she is. Can you handle both?"

Finley swallowed hard. "I'll try."

"I can help, Lee!" Alexander cried, jumping to his feet.

"No, you finish listening to the story. I'll be fine."

Much to his surprise, he *was* fine.

He gave his tail to one girl to play with while he changed the other, very grateful to Alexander for showing him how to do a diaper properly the day before, and then switched them places. Atlanta shifted into her winged-wolf puppy form and tried to attack his tail.

And so it continued for the rest of the day, Finley overcoming any challenges thrown at him in his own way. By the time parents started arriving for pick-up, he was exhausted, but honestly impressed with himself.

Maybe kids aren't so bad.

He waved goodbye to a yawning Atlanta cuddled in her imposing father's arms.

Maybe I could manage to envision a life with Artemis and her kid.

He gave himself a shake. That was unlikely. Just because he'd gotten on well enough with these kids under Hestia's supervision didn't mean that he was ready—or willing—to be around a kid he didn't know.

A black sedan drove up to the front of the daycare.

"That's Alexander's mom's car," Hestia said. "Get your things, sweetie, and I'll walk you out."

Finley was handing Lyta blocks for her to stack in her artistic representation of a tower when she let out an explosive fart. And the smell didn't dissipate.

"Uhhhh, Hestia?" Finley called. "Not sure I can deal with this one."

"Oh, fiddlesticks. Can you bring

Alexander out to his mother, please?" Hestia said, scooping the baby up under both arms and turning her. "Yup, a complete blowout. I think you need to be moved up a size in diapers, missy."

"Ready to go, young man?" Finley asked Alexander as Hestia vanished down the hallway to the bigger bathroom.

"I'm not a young man," Alexander said.

"What are you then?"

"I'm Alexander."

"Can't argue with that. Let's go see your mom."

Alexander took Finley's hand, his tiny fingers wrapping around only one of Finley's. His heart melted.

At the car, he finally looked up at the

driver.

It was a man.

"Hang on, bud," Finley told Alexander.

The door opened and the man stepped out, leaning against the car. He crossed his arms, revealing a snake tattoo on his hand that disappeared under the sleeve of his shirt. "I'll just pop him in the back. Ms. Chase hired me to pick up her son today."

Finley's instincts were screaming at him not to trust this guy.

"I'm just going to go check with Hestia about that. Any change to the usual pick-up procedure would have been called in." He had no idea if he was right about that, but it seemed like a logical thing to do.

"Ah, that won't be a problem. I'll make things easy for you and get him settled in his seat." The man moved swiftly, taking Alexander by the upper arm before Finley was even aware that he'd left the side of the car.

Cursing himself for being so lax and letting Alexander loosen his grip, Finley sprang into action. The expression of terror on the little boy's face was enough to let him know that this was not a normal situation.

"The boy is staying with me," Finley said firmly, sliding his body between Alexander and the car and grabbing the man's wrist.

He used his fingers to apply pressure between the bones of the wrist. The nerves would stop working properly in three, two, one— The instant the man's hand loosened on the boy's arm, Finley pulled Alexander free.

"Back to the house, *now*," he ordered the boy. "Ring the doorbell and get inside."

"Ms. Chase is going to be angry," the man said, lowering into a crouch.

"For some reason, I sincerely doubt that," Finley growled, keeping himself between the man and Alexander, who was following his instructions. "Are we going to dance, or what?"

The man moved so fast that only Finley's instincts could follow, dodging around the dragon shifter and trying to get at the boy. Finley reached out at the last second and grabbed him by the arm.

"Oh no you don't."

The man grinned and shifted into snake form, slithering out of Finley's grasp and whipping toward Alexander, who was still outside the door.

"Not on my watch." Finley shifted into dragon form between one heartbeat and the next, leaping on top of the giant snake and throwing it back against the car. His scales rippled as he prowled toward the snake, gaze fixed on his prey.

"You will not touch this child. You will tell your boss from jail that he is off-limits. Do you understand me?"

The snake hissed a reply, venom dripping from his fangs. It weaved back and forth before launching at Finley's face, wrapping itself around his muzzle and striking at his vulnerable eyes.

Fortunately, Finley was prepared for

this tactic, and had covered his eyes with the transparent inner lid, just as thick as his scales. The fangs could not get through, and while the snake was distracted by that, Finley pinned its body to the ground.

"Alexander, what— Oh my goodness!" Hestia shrieked.

Finley spoke without moving his eyes from the still squirming snake. "Since you've got Alexander, I'm going to take this wannabe kidnapper to the police station. See how he likes being in jail," he growled.

"Thank you, Finley. I'm very glad you were here."

"You would have managed." Finley scooped up the snake in his claws. "I'll be back. I'm sure Maddie would like to hear all the details about this little encounter."

"Most definitely."

Finley leapt into the air, wings catching an updraft, and soared over Purgatory.

"Take a look around, little snake. This will be the last taste of freedom for you for a long time."

He was greeted outside the police station by a cop who tied a chain around the snake's neck, forcing him to change back into a human.

After a long debrief at the police station, Finley returned to Maddie's daycare, to be greeted with a hug.

"Thank you," Maddie said tearfully. "Sorry, pregnancy hormones. We'll be extra careful from now on."

"You would've done the same thing if you'd been here."

"Neither of us can change into a dragon," Hestia said definitively.

Finley grinned. "You're right. *He's* lucky I was here."

CHAPTER FIVE

"THAT'S IT! I'VE had enough!" bellowed a voice through her noise-canceling office door.

Artemis looked up from Charon's revised proposal, a headache developing behind her right temple, and blinked in surprise at the time on the wall clock opposite her.

Is that really the time?

She pressed a button on the

messenger system between her office and Luna's desk just outside it. "Luna, I've got to go or I'll be late to pick up Alexander. I'll finish this up tomorrow morning." She stuck a sticky note where she'd stopped reading and stacked the papers neatly back into their folder.

The door burst open and Artemis didn't even look up from arranging her desk when she said, "Thank you, Luna. If you could put that away in the safe, please, I'd be very grateful."

Twin thumps on her desk made her head fly up, meeting the angry gaze of Mercury. "You!" he spat. "I've had enough of your deflection. Tell me what you plan to do with this 'expansion' of yours!"

Artemis regarded him coolly. He

looked particularly disheveled today; no tie, shirt completely untucked, hair in disarray. His fists were propped on her desk, his face was getting redder and redder the longer she didn't answer him.

She ignored him and looked out her door in concern at Luna, who was standing and staring at nothing. "Remove your thrall from my assistant," she said in a low voice, one she usually only reserved for Alexander when he was especially naughty or the board members when they were being particularly difficult. Alexander rarely heard that tone from her. The board members couldn't say the same.

"Or what?" Mercury sneered.

"You don't want to know. *Now.*"

"I could put you in my thrall and you

would tell me everything I want to know," Mercury threatened, playing with a silver chain that hung out of his open shirt collar.

"I'd like to see you try." Artemis smirked, crossing her arms.

Mercury made some gestures and pushed a force toward her.

Artemis shook off the compulsion as if it were a spiderweb. "That was fun. Release my assistant and maybe we can talk like civilized people."

The redness of rage had shifted into embarrassment, and Mercury turned away from her, apparently shaken. Seconds later, Luna came running into the office.

"I'm sorry, Miss Chase, I couldn't stop him!" Luna cried, wringing her hands apologetically.

"Nothing to worry about. Please take this file and put it in the safe for me." Artemis handed her the Charon file. "I won't be long with Mercury."

Once Luna had left the office with the confidential file, Artemis turned the full force of her piercing silver eyes on the hapless God. "Whatever reason you might have had barging into my office and enthralling my assistant, it's not good enough. I don't care if I bulldozed your *house* to the ground, this little display of a temper tantrum was not worth it for you. My *son* behaves better than you do when he doesn't get his way, and he's not even three years old."

Mercury flushed even more. "I'll cut to the chase." Artemis shot him a dirty look for the pun. "I heard you were looking into getting into the shipping business, horning in on my turf."

"Are you serious?" Artemis rolled her eyes. "Not only was that a ridiculous reason, but that rumor doesn't even have a single grain of truth to it."

"But you *are* looking into expanding your business?" Mercury asked shrewdly.

"I plan on remaining in *banking*," Artemis emphasized clearly. "Whoever your source is needs to get their facts straight. Now, if you'll excuse me, I'm late to pick up my son because of this little charade." Her words were polite, but her tone allowed no room for argument.

"If I ever hear otherwise..." Mercury

slunk out of her office, metaphorical tail between his legs, threat sounding empty.

"Right. I hope to never see you again," Artemis growled. She grabbed her purse and locked the door behind her.

***

The drive to the daycare had never seemed so long. The shadows were lengthening by the time she pulled up in front of the little building and put the car in park. When she rang the doorbell, the voices inside got louder.

The door swung open revealing Maddie. "Thank goodness you're here!" she said, relieved.

"I'm sorry I'm late. Is everything okay?" Maddie shook her head, expression somber, and Artemis's heart sank to her toes. "Where's Alexander? What's wrong?"

"Mom!" Alexander called from the living space.

Artemis breathed a sigh of relief when she saw him. He looked fine, although his eyes were red from crying. She picked him up as soon as he got close enough. "I'm sorry I'm late, darling. I should have called, but I got caught up unexpectedly. There's no need for tears." She hugged him tightly as he buried his face in her neck.

"Lee stopped a bad man from taking me," Alexander whispered.

"*What?*" Artemis gasped, her legs giving out on her. She sank into a chair and looked up at the two women for an explanation.

"I was at an appointment," Maddie said, wringing her hands. "And Jaden's brother was here. He took Alexander out when Hestia saw a car that looked like yours drive up. But when a man got out, he sent Alexander back to the house. The driver shifted into a snake—"

"Lee turned into a blue dragon!" Alexander said excitedly. "He's so *big*! He stopped the bad man from getting me and then took him away to be locked up."

Hestia nodded. "That sums it up nicely."

"Thank goodness for Jaden's brother," Artemis whispered, petting Alexander's hair.

"Lee," Alexander corrected her.

Artemis pressed a kiss to his

forehead. "Lee," she repeated. "Was any reason given as to *why* Alexander was targeted?"

"Not that we're aware of, but he's not back from the police station. Maybe the snake talked there. Can you think of anyone who has something to gain by taking him?"

Artemis started to say no, but the image of Mercury popped into her head suddenly.

Would he?

He had a pretty flimsy excuse today, and it delayed her from leaving the office long enough that she wasn't able to pick Alexander up on time...

She shook her head, a sick feeling in her stomach. "I don't think anyone would stoop so low as to kidnap my child," she said shakily.

"Think about it," Hestia advised. "If you think of anyone, tell us and we'll update the police report."

"Thank you. Thank Lee for me too." Artemis shakily got to her feet, not wanting to let go of Alexander, but needing to get him home and cuddle him more comfortably. "Come along, sweetheart. Why don't we order dinner and play with Elati until bedtime?"

"Yes, please! Can we have chicken nuggets?"

"I suppose so," Artemis said with a half-smile at his care-givers.

****

Later, Artemis sat in one of the lounge chairs in her backyard, watching

Alexander and her fawn, Elati, chase each other around the garden.

Alexander found a ball under a large plant leaf and started kicking it. Elati pranced after him, kicking up her heels and tossing her head in play. Whenever she got too close, Alexander would scoop up the ball and run further away with it, chortling with gleeful laughter that Artemis found infectious.

"Why don't you try kicking the ball *to* Elati?" she suggested. "Let her play with it too."

Alexander's kick went wide, but Elati bounced after the ball, prancing around it and angling her head in different ways to look at it properly.

Artemis stifled her giggle, wanting to see what would happen.

"Kick it back, Lati!" Alexander shouted excitedly. "You can do it!"

The fawn bent awkwardly, spindly legs splayed wide, and pushed the ball a bit with the top of her nose.

Alexander fell over laughing.

Artemis smiled. "Good girl, Elati," she encouraged.

The fawn pranced a bit and headbutted the ball again before licking it.

"We don't put toys in our mouths," Alexander scolded through his giggles.

Elati finished pushing the ball over to him, and Alexander mirrored her position to push the ball back to her.

Bath tonight.

Artemis absentmindedly watched her son rub his face and hair against the grass. She could feel the moonrise starting deep in her bones. "All right, sweetheart. Two minutes before we have to go in."

"But Moooom!" Alexander complained.

Artemis raised her eyebrow and Alexander quieted.

"If I talk, I don't get to play," he said.

"Good remembering. You get a bath tonight, so you have something to look forward to."

"Yay! Can we go in now?"

Artemis stifled a laugh. "Sure, if that's what you'd like. Say goodnight to Elati."

"Night Lati!" Alexander skipped into the house.

***

Artemis got almost as wet as Alexander during his bath, something which she shrugged off. She was going to have a shower as soon as he was in bed anyway.

"Story?" Alexander begged, once he was in his pajamas and tucked into bed, holding his stuffed teddy bear.

"Let me think. Have I told you the story about the Moon Goddess before?" Artemis asked, knowing what his answer would be.

"Yes! That's you! Tell me again!" Alexander bounced a bit on the mattress.

"That doesn't look like you're calm enough for a story," Artemis hedged, and Alexander wiggled under the covers until only his big gray eyes peeped out. She ruffled his blond hair with one hand. "The Moon Goddess was lonely. Her brother, Apollo, was the Sun God, and she rarely ever saw him, because he drove the chariot that pulled the sun across the sky, while she did the same for the moon.

"One evening, she looked down upon the Earth and saw some young men and women bathing in a pool of shining silver. It was the reflection of her moon on the water below. She so yearned to join them, that she took a ribbon of moonlight and slid down it like a slide, right into the midst of the group!

"They were very nice to the Goddess and invited her to go swimming with them. She had so much fun that she joined them every full moon after that, dancing and rejoicing in the moonlight."

"I love you, Mom," Alexander said, and yawned wide. He lifted his arms up. "Kiss?"

"Of course darling." She pressed a gentle kiss to his soft cheek. "I love you so much. May you dream of whatever you love most."

"Night." His eyes closed and he squeezed his bear tighter.

Artemis checked that the monitor was turned on and left the room, closing the door behind her with a sigh of relief. She loved her son more than anything else in the world, but it was nice to have time just for herself.

A quick detour into her own room to strip out of her clothing and slip into a freshly cleaned cotton robe before she grabbed the other end of the monitor. So as not to keep Alexander awake, she went to the extra bathroom on the lower level of the house, as far from his bedroom as possible.

She kept the water cool, not wanting to overheat her skin before the even colder temperatures of the pond below her fountain. Artemis scrubbed her body thoroughly, first with unscented soap, and then with her hands, removing all the suds. She didn't want to injure any of the wildlife because of carelessness. Once she was certain she was clean, she stepped out and wrapped the cotton robe around her body.

A quick glance at the screen of the monitor showed Alexander asleep on his belly, his bum up in the air, holding onto his bear's paw. She nodded to herself; unless he had a nightmare, he'd sleep through the night.

Barefoot, Artemis checked that the front door was locked before heading out the back door to her garden. The privacy hedges surrounding the yard meant that she couldn't see her neighbors, but neither could they see her. The yard extended into the forest, where Elati lived. The fawn was still in the yard, though.

"Did you know I'd be back out because of the moon?" Artemis cooed to the animal, putting the monitor down on the table and going to her pet. "What a clever girl you are!" She let Elati butt against her side before smoothing her hand down the side of the fawn's neck, the springy fur soothing to the touch. "You'll watch over Alexander while I'm bathing, won't you? Is he *your* pet?" She chuckled at the idea and backed away, just enough to move without bumping into Elati.

She draped the cotton robe over the back of the chair and walked nude across the soft clover that made up the lawn to the large pond. There were rocks the height of her knee around the edge to prevent Alexander from accidentally falling in. She knelt on one, the hard surface smooth to the touch, and dipped her hand into the water. The moon was almost completely reflected on the top, the ripples that she made slowly traveling across to the other side.

Artemis pulled at a beam of

moonlight, shaping it into a handle that she then used to climb into the pond. She shivered a little; even though she'd prepared herself for the temperature, it was another thing to feel the cold water lapping against her skin.

The koi fish she kept ventured over to greet her, their fins tickling her ribs.

"Hello, you pretty things," she greeted them, letting them bite at her fingertips. "I think you'll find some algae or something more to your taste than me."

The deep pull in her bones heralded the full moon's appearance in the pond. Artemis closed her eyes and floated, basking in the light, pulling its strength and beauty into her soul until she felt full.

She tipped her face up until she was

looking directly into the moonbeams. "I glowed after orgasm last night," she whispered. "Do you know why?"

A pulse of energy shone down on her, her heart filled to bursting from the love she felt inside it.

"Is that it?" she murmured, more to herself than to the moon. "I felt a connection with him?" A tear trickled down her cheek and she shook her head to remove it. "But he ran at the mention of my son. He can't be my soulmate!"

The moonlight warmed briefly.

"All right. I'll try." Artemis wanted to curl in on herself, wrap herself in fluffy blankets, but she was bathing in water and moonbeam, fully exposed. She couldn't ignore what the moon was telling her. That her heart was already won, that she needed to trust herself, that everything would be all right in time.

The pull of the moon lessened; it was leaving the pond.

"Thank you," Artemis whispered to it. "I'll make you proud."

CHAPTER SIX

SEVERAL DAYS LATER, Finley was feeling more confident with the kids at the daycare. It was thunderstorming, the rain hitting the large glass door into the backyard with a pattering that echoed throughout the living room.

The boys were chasing each other around the room, shouting at the top of their lungs. The excitement got the attention of the younger girls, and

Atlanta shifted into her winged-wolf form to join in the fun, yipping shrilly and letting her tongue hang out as she raced after the boys.

"It's way too early to start lunch," Hestia said, shaking her head. "But someone is going to get hurt if this keeps up."

"A story?" Finley suggested.

"It's worth a shot." Hestia scanned the titles of the books on the shelf. "Ah, here we go." Without saying a word, she took the book over to the rocking chair in the corner and sat down, opening the book on her lap.

Damien stopped so abruptly that Alexander crashed into him. "Are you going to read us a story?" he asked eagerly.

"If you'd like me to," Hestia replied. She winked up at Finley as the children gathered around her chair quietly, all humanoid now.

***

The rain had petered down to a drizzle by the time Damien had to leave for an appointment.

"It's time for your naps, girls," Hestia said cheerfully, putting Lyta on her hip. "Finley, you good?"

"Alexander and I will be fine," he said. "I thought I might teach him a new game."

"What game?" Alexander asked excitedly, jumping from one foot to the other. "Is it hard?"

Finley shrugged. "It can be. I find it

fun. It's called Mastermind. It's all about logic."

"What's logic?"

"It's reasoning. The *why* you do things." Finley could tell he'd lost the kid. "Don't worry. It'll make sense once we play."

He brought Alexander over to the main table and pulled out the modeling clay in different colors. "I'm going to come up with a pattern of colors and hide them under this piece of paper. You have to guess which colors they are. I'll give you clues. Why don't we start with two colors?"

"Okay!"

Finley opened the jars, the sweet-sour scent of the clay filling the air the instant the first lid was removed. "Close your eyes." He took tiny bits from the pink and green jars and covered the little balls with the piece of paper. "Ready to guess?"

Alexander opened his eyes and bounced a little in his chair. "What do I do?"

"Take a pinch of clay from each jar that you think I've hidden," Finley suggested.

Alexander chose green and yellow.

"Excellent start," Finley said approvingly. "Now, I'm going to give you a white piece of clay to show that you got one right. The other one is wrong."

"But which one is right?" Alexander asked, frowning.

"That's for you to figure out," Finley replied. "Try replacing one of them with another color."

Alexander chose red and took away the green.

"You have no white pieces now." Finley removed the white clay. "What does that tell you?"

Alexander picked up the green. "This was one!" he exclaimed triumphantly.

"Very good. Anything else?"

"It's not red or yellow."

"Great. Keep going." Finley was impressed by how fast the boy caught on to the game.

Alexander chose blue next and finally pink. He looked so proud of himself when Finley showed him that he'd gotten the answer right. "Again! Again!" the little boy chanted, sliding out of his chair and doing a row of somersaults across the floor.

"Do you want me to hide three colors now?"

"Yes!"

They played five more times, increasing the difficulty to a specific order of four colors, by the time that Hestia joined them. She raised her eyebrows—surprised or impressed, Finley wasn't certain—before busying herself with organizing a craft for once the girls awoke.

Finley basked in the quiet intensity that Alexander was radiating, all his focus on the little colored dots of clay as he tried to figure out the code. To be perfectly honest, Finley was seriously impressed that the little boy was not only wanting to continue playing the game, but was succeeding at it. He knew adults who had trouble with the amount of concentration needed.

Only the return of Damien took Alexander away from the new game. Finley had a sneaking suspicion that it would be highly sought after in the future, just like every other new thing introduced to children that age.

After lunch, the skies cleared, and Hestia suggested that they all go outside for some fresh air. They helped the kids put on splash pants and boots and headed out into the soggy backyard.

Finley leaned against the side of the building as he watched the kids gleefully stomp in puddles, splashing much higher than the protection of the waistband of the protective pants. "Why did we bother to stuff them into those plastic things if they're going to be wet from head to toe anyway?" he asked Hestia.

"Because this way, there's a chance that their underwear will stay dry." Hestia chuckled. "Not much of a chance, but a slim one nonetheless."

"I suppose that's worth it." Finley offered a tiny smile.

Unfortunately, the toddlers could get their diapers wet in other ways, and Hestia had to bring Lyta inside to change her, leaving Finley alone with the other three charges.

He was "helping" Atlanta build a sand and mud castle when a loud shriek met his ears.

"*Lee!*"

Finley leapt to his feet in a heartbeat to see a pair of harpy-like shifters, each holding Alexander by an arm. "Stay!" he ordered Atlanta, running as fast as he could toward the winged thugs. At the end of the yard, he leapt into the air, shifting into his dragon form with hardly a thought.

Suddenly *much* larger than the would-be kidnappers, he caught up to them easily. He carefully wrapped one claw-tipped hand around Alexander's tiny body before growling deep in his chest.

The harpies shrieked in terror to see him, not having noticed the giant dragon sneak up on them while they were fighting to keep their grip on the struggling boy. They let go of Alexander and sped away, flapping their wings as fast as they could go.

"I've got you," Finley crooned to the sobbing boy in his hand, back-winging swiftly, his large bat-like wings cutting through the air with the ease of practice. He landed in the backyard, which suddenly felt too small for him, and gently placed Alexander on the grass. "Go inside, all of you," he ordered. "I've got some people to bring to justice."

Tail lashing, he leapt skyward again, accompanied by a small black figure.

He was two wingbeats away from the daycare when he noticed his shadow. He sighed and shook his large head, but slowed. The harpies were too far ahead of him at this point, and there was no way he could bring Atlanta back and *then* catch them. "Come on, little one," he said to the winged-wolf toddler. "Good job keeping up with me."

The toddler yipped excitedly and executed some aerial acrobatics between Finley's forearms.

"It's time to land," Finley said sternly, nudging her rear with the tip of his nose. "Stay with me."

This time, when he landed, he shifted back to his human form right away. He caught Atlanta and strode quickly to the building with her in his arms. Once inside, he scanned the faces anxiously, relieved when he saw that everyone else was all right.

"I didn't know she'd chase me," he said apologetically to Hestia, who hurried over to him to take the child.

"She's fine."

"Of course she is," Hestia said firmly. "She was with you." She raised her eyebrow in question, but Finley shook his head minutely. Any details that she wanted would have to wait until the kids weren't listening. "Why don't we get all of you changed and then you can watch a movie?"

"Yay!"

Once the movie was on, Finley and Hestia went into the little office, but kept the door open so they could keep an eye on the puppy pile of children in the big room.

"What happened?" Hestia asked.

Finley told her, leaving out no details, and she wrote everything down.

"Did you catch them?"

He shook his head. "I'm not sure I would have been able to catch them even without Atlanta's assistance," he said with a wry twist to his mouth. "My first priority was to get Alexander safely back to you. That gave them quite the head start."

"As much as an aerial battle would have been amazing to watch," Hestia murmured under her breath.

"I'm a lot slower when I'm a dragon," Finley said. "Turning and acrobatics are a lot more difficult for me in the air."

"You could shift to turn around and then shift back," Hestia suggested.

Finley's jaw dropped, both a little surprised that he hadn't thought of that option and that matronly Hestia had suggested it, when he caught the twinkle in her eye. "You are a very interesting woman," he said with a chuckle. "All right, next time I get the chance to fight in mid-air, I'll try your suggestion.

Hestia blushed as if he'd praised her. "Only if you don't get hurt in the process."

Shrugging, Finley said, "I get hurt all the time. Nothing that a little sleep won't heal." He nodded at the account he'd given her. "Can we make a copy of that for the police?"

"That's my plan. Go over it, make sure you haven't missed anything, especially in your description of the harpies, and then we'll call up Chloe. She'll know who to contact to give this to."

"Okay."

Hestia left him in the little room to read. When he was done, he returned to the main room to see Alexander sobbing quietly in Hestia's full bosom. "Hey now, what's all this?" Finley asked softly, running his hand over soft curls and a sturdy back.

"He's feeling a little overwhelmed," Hestia replied. "Now that you're out, I'm going to take him back to the nap room."

"No no no no!" Alexander's voice rose with each repetition. He twisted away from Hestia and threw himself at Finley, who caught him, barely. "Want *Lee!*"

"Uhhh, I guess I'll take him to the nap room?" Finley said questioningly to Hestia.

She nodded with a smile, so Finley carried the boy away from the brightly singing television and into the last room at the end of the hall.

Alexander's sobs had quieted down, but he was still shaking uncontrollably as Finley lowered himself into the sturdy rocking chair next to the cots. He arranged the boy's legs to drape across his own, his arm draped protectively around Alexander's back. "Deep breaths," Finley murmured, automatically slowing his own breathing. "We're going to do a calming exercise, okay? Give me your hands."

Slowly, Finley brought each of Alexander's fingers to its match on the other hand, until all five were touching. "Now it's your turn," he said.

The concentration required took Alexander's mind off of crying, until finally he stopped altogether.

"Good." Finley gently held both hands in one of his, marveling at how tiny the boy was. He gestured around the room with his free hand. "What can you see?"

"A bed." Alexander sniffed and pulled one hand free to wipe his nose on the back of it.

"Good. What's special about this bed that you can see?"

"There's no pillow."

"You're right. That's kinda odd, isn't it?"

"Maddie said we don't need pillows for naps."

"Fascinating. What else can you tell me about the bed?"

"The blanket is blue."

"Nice. That's my favorite color, didn't

you know that?" Finley asked.

Alexander looked up at him. "Is that because you're a blue dragon?"

"You betcha." Finley booped Alexander's nose with a finger, making the boy giggle. "That's better. Whenever you're feeling like you can't catch your breath and you're crying, find a quiet corner and press each finger to its pair. You can do that many times, until you're calm. Then find one object and look at it really closely. Find one special thing about it. Do you think you can do that?"

"Yes." Alexander nodded solemnly.

"Do you want to finish your movie now?"

"Can I sit with you?"

"Of course."

***

Maddie returned not long after, but Finley stayed until the end of the movie because of his promise to Alexander.

After getting a tight hug from Maddie, Finley left the daycare. He had just enough time to go home to grab his gear and a quick bite to eat before his match at Valhalla's Throne.

He checked the match board when he arrived to see that he'd be fighting Emerald. He nodded thoughtfully. She was lithe, fast, and controlled. Probably the fighter who had the best chance of beating him, if he was honest.

Once in his private ready room, he got changed and rolled his dice; he was to attempt to win his match. Finley headed for the backstage to stretch and loosen up his muscles.

"Are you ready to get trounced?" Emerald greeted him.

"You wish," Finley replied with a snort, sitting on the floor and sticking his legs out in a V. He bent over his right leg. "You might be good, but I'm going to take home the win tonight." They'd had this conversation before every match. It was almost ritualistic. He smirked. "Maybe you could beat me if you kept an eye on your left hook."

"My left hook is perfectly fine, thank you very much," Emerald said with a sniff. "*You* need to watch your balance after your right kick."

Finley's grin widened. That was his normal "weakness" that allowed him to lose credibly. "I've been practicing."

"Against those brutes you call your brothers?"

Finley switched sides, stretching out over his left leg. "Sometimes. Mostly, though, I practice my forms on my own. Hey, can I ask you something?"

Emerald raised a perfectly sculpted eyebrow. He was deviating from their script. "I can't promise an answer."

"Fair." Finley lowered his voice and leaned forward between his legs. "Have you seen any guys with a snake tattoo on their wrist? Or know any harpy-like shifters?"

Emerald looked thoughtful. "I see all types at the convenience store. Why do you ask?"

He lowered his voice to barely a whisper. "The snake tried to kidnap a little boy at Maddie's daycare the other day. You know, Jaden's mate? And this afternoon, two harpies snatched him out of the backyard."

"No shit!" Emerald's eyes widened. "I'll let you know if I find anything out, and I'll keep my lips sealed about this."

"Thank you."

They finished their stretching in companionable silence.

"Please put your hands together for Finley 'Finn' McKellen and Emerald 'Gem' Haviston!" the announcer hyped up the crowd.

Finley fist-bumped Emerald and then they walked on stage.

CHAPTER SEVEN

ARTEMIS LEFT WORK early for an appointment at ButterNut Bakery. It was well after the lunch rush and not quite time for dinner, so she and Demi and Hera were able to sit down together at one of the little tables with only minor interruptions from customers.

"What's the theme?" Demi asked, flicking her pen against her notepad.

"Theme?" Artemis repeated.

"Birthday?"

"Yes, of course it's his birthday," Hera said. "But what sort of theme do you want to tie things together? What does he like?"

"He likes everything," Artemis replied, feeling a little like she didn't know her own child. "He likes to help me cook?"

"We could do a Pizza Party theme," Demi suggested.

"Oooh, and then the kids could make their own little pizzas as a snack!" Hera added.

"The cake could look like a pizza. And the decor could all be pizza shaped." Demi started scribbling their ideas down. "Okay, that's a start. Let's come up with something else to compare."

Artemis felt a little like her head was

spinning from the rapidity of the conversation. When she realized both bakers were looking at her expectantly, she scrambled for another idea. "He likes to do crafts, I guess?"

"Hmm..." Demi said thoughtfully. "Definitely a craft table no matter what. We'll get Maddie in on that. I've always wanted to try making a pencil cake."

"And the snacks can be decorated to look like craft supplies," Hera suggested.

"What happens if they try to eat the real craft supplies?" Artemis asked, alarmed. "Maybe that's not a good idea. How about animals? Alexander adores Elati."

Demi dragged her pen through the craft idea and wrote the new one down. "I can make the cake look like a meadow, maybe with little animal toys on top? And we can have a pinata, the snacks can look like different animal foods, like dog biscuits that are actually cookies."

"That's a great idea," Artemis said, relieved to have picked a theme that she hadn't known she needed. "I love it."

"Leave it with us," Hera reassured her. "This birthday party is going to be awesome!"

"I have no doubts."

"Remind me how many people are going to be there," Demi asked.

"It's just the daycare kids and their families," Artemis said, counting on her fingers. "Maddie, Hestia, the three kids and their parents... That's eleven. Plus Jaden, his brothers, and you two make sixteen."

"And yourself," Hera pointed out.

"Right. And Luna. Eighteen. I haven't heard from Alexander's father, but I doubt he'll make an appearance." Artemis crossed her arms and bit back a "good riddance". Just because she couldn't stand the man and what he'd done to her son didn't mean she had to broadcast it to everyone.

"That's a good number," Demi said, distracting her from the dark turn of her thoughts.

"I've been thinking about hiring some extra security," Artemis said hesitantly.

The sisters exchanged glances. "I heard about the attempts to kidnap Alexander from Augustine," Hera said comfortingly. "I don't blame you in the slightest."

"But?" Artemis prompted.

Hera hesitated. "Will it be necessary for this party? There will be a lot of adults there to keep an eye on the kids, and everyone is someone you know or Maddie knows very well."

Artemis stayed silent, rubbing her fingertips over a ridge in the table. "I was actually thinking about hiring them for the daycare on a regular basis. If I do nothing and something happens, I'll never be able to forgive myself. And while I trust Maddie and Hestia implicitly, neither of them are really the fighting sort. I was just lucky that Lee was there both times."

"Then you should hire some people." Hera shrugged. "Peace of mind is better than regretting it later."

Some tension left Artemis's body. "Thanks. I think I needed to hear that I wasn't overreacting."

"This is your child. You aren't overreacting," Demi said firmly. "I'll make you a list of people that would be good for that."

"Oh, would you? Thank you so much!" It really was a weight off her mind.

"We'll contact you if we have any further questions," Hera said, getting to her feet with a smile.

"That's it?" To be fair, Artemis didn't really know what went into planning a party. That's why she hired people to do it for her.

"That's it for now. We've got a pretty

good idea of what you want," Demi said. "Why don't you take the rest of the day to relax?"

Artemis glanced at the clock. There were over two hours before she had to pick Alexander up from daycare. "I might do just that," she said with a chuckle. "I need some 'me' time."

"Damn right you do," Hera said vehemently. "We are Goddesses and we need pampering!"

Feeling giddy, like she was skipping school, Artemis left the bakery. She called Luna to tell her where she was going and that she wouldn't be back in today while she walked to her car.

Luna, of course, approved of the plan. "You've been working too hard lately. Relax. You deserve it."

"I don't pay you enough," Artemis said.

"You pay me just fine, but I wouldn't say no to a raise," Luna replied cheekily.

"I'll look into it."

"Tomorrow."

Artemis turned her car toward Psyche's Spa. Her Goddess energy might have been replenished thanks to her moonlit dip, but her physical energy was drained. A trip to the spa was definitely in order.

"How can I help you?" greeted the girl at the counter when Artemis walked in.

"This is super last minute. I don't have an appointment," Artemis began.

"Not to worry. We take walk-ins," the girl replied, her voice chipper.

"I have to leave in just under two

hours. Other than a massage, what can I get done in that time?"

"We can fit in a mani-pedi without a problem. A mud bath might take a little too long. A facial, if you want. Hair conditioning. What interests you?"

"I think I'll go with the nails after the massage, if that's possible." It had been way too long since she'd had time or energy to do anything fancier than trim her nails.

"And how long do you want the massage?" the girl asked, typing on her computer.

"Is an hour too long?"

"Not at all."

"Fantastic."

"There are clean robes in each locker. Pick one and leave your clothes behind.

There are signs that will direct you to the massage rooms. Preference of gender?"

"Female, please," Artemis requested. She didn't think she could handle a man's touch after Finley had made her fall apart so thoroughly such a short time ago.

She found the robes in the lockers just as they were described and changed quickly, eager to get her massage started. There was calming music playing quietly over hidden speakers, setting the mood for relaxation. The color scheme of muted greens, grays, and creams added to the effect.

A woman greeted her at the entrance to the massage rooms. "Good day, Artemis. I am Psyche and I will be your masseuse today."

"The owner?" Artemis asked, surprised.

"I love to help out in the massage rooms. I got my license before I started this place, and keep up to date on techniques monthly," Psyche replied.

"I wasn't questioning your abilities," Artemis reassured her.

"I didn't think you were." Psyche smiled. She gestured inside one of the darkened rooms. "Shall we begin?"

"Yes, please."

"Please remove your robe and lay on your stomach on the bed. Here is a sheet for your modesty, if you wish." Psyche backed out of the room, closing the door as she went. "I'll be with you in two minutes."

Artemis hung her robe on the hook

on the back of the door before getting on the bed, ignoring the sheet. She admired the lush orchid in a square vase beside a tea light directly in front of her. Looking around the room, she saw that there wasn't much else in here besides a small table with a bottle of lotion. The music from in the change room continued in here, but the lighting was much dimmer; reminiscent of a candlelit dinner.

A knock sounded on the door. "Are you ready in here?" Psyche asked. When Artemis answered, she opened the door fully and entered. She made no comment regarding Artemis's choice to be nude and went straight to the lotion. "I will start with the large muscle groups in your back and legs before I move on to the smaller muscles of your neck and arms. How often have you had a massage?"

"I can't remember the last time I had one," Artemis admitted.

"If I press too hard, let me know immediately."

By the time Psyche removed her hands from Artemis's skin for the last time, Artemis didn't remember much about her massage. It felt like she had entered a dream-like state as Psyche worked each muscle into a relaxed, boneless, mass.

"You don't have to rush. Sit up slowly and take your time," Psyche said at the end of the hour. "Once you feel ready, the nail salon is to the left outside the door. You can stay in your robe or you can change back into your clothes, it's up to you."

"Thank you so much," Artemis said, her voice muffled from her cheek being pressed against the bed. "That was amazing. You are incredible at this. Can I ask for you next time I come?"

"You can ask, but it would work better if you made an appointment," Psyche teased.

"I'll try to remember that." Artemis lay on the bed, fully relaxed, for several minutes after Psyche had left the room. Her limbs and head felt heavy. At last, she got slowly to her feet, wiped a trickle of drool from the side of her mouth, and pulled on her robe.

The manicure and pedicure also involved massaging of her hands and feet. She chose a soft pink polish for her nails.

By the end of her appointment, she had decided that she had to come back, at least every two weeks. She felt less stressed and more prepared to take on the days ahead.

On her way out to her car, she called Luna again. "I'm bringing you with me next time," she said in greeting.

Luna chuckled. "I accept. Was that all you were calling to say?"

"Yes. Heading to pick up Alexander now."

"See you tomorrow."

One of the things that Artemis had thought about during the massage was how she felt like she didn't know her son.

What did he like to play with?

What was his favorite color?

Was it still green?

She decided that the best way to get to know her son again would be to take him somewhere new and fun. He'd never been to the human world, and he'd be safer, since it was unlikely that whoever was after him would think about following them there.

Plan decided upon, Artemis went to pick up Alexander from daycare. He abandoned the train he was playing with to run at her legs and hug them.

"You don't get here until after Damien *and* Lyta are gone!" Alexander said.

"I'm sorry, do you want me to leave?" Artemis teased.

"No! Are you here to see Maddie?"

"I'm here to get you. And I thought

maybe we could go somewhere new. What do you think about that?"

Alexander's jaw dropped open. "Yes!" he squeaked.

"Tidy up first, please," Artemis said, and Alexander scampered away to put the train tracks in their designated bin.

"He's an angel, you know that, right?" Maddie said. "We love having him here."

"He loves being here," Artemis replied, her heart swelling with pride. "I thought it would be nice to do something different together today."

"Oh, totally." Maddie rubbed the swell of her belly. "Hey, can I ask you a question?"

"Sure."

"Did you ever regret being pregnant?"

Artemis glanced over to where

Alexander was finishing up and lowered her voice. "Many times. But once I held him, I knew I had made the right choice." She frowned. "Is Jaden having second thoughts?"

Maddie chuckled. "Definitely not. He's very eager to meet our little one."

"What's up then? You're going to be a fantastic mother."

"It just feels so soon. Jaden and I only barely moved in together and now we're welcoming a baby? We didn't have much time to just be the two of us."

"I see." Artemis tried not to be jealous, but it was hard. "Your vision of your life isn't the same as reality."

Maddie blushed. "I guess you're right."

"Enjoy what you've got. When your

little one is grown, you'll have time with Jaden." Artemis smiled. "And do you really think that Augustine and Hera wouldn't babysit?"

"That is an excellent point."

"Mom! I'm ready!" Alexander shouted, bouncing up to them.

"Great!" Artemis held her hand out to him, her heart melting when his tiny fingers slipped into her own.

She was honestly impressed as she drove out of Purgatory. Alexander hadn't asked her even once about their destination. She drove through the portal meant for cars, coming out in the bright sunshine of downtown Los Angeles. The portal was disguised as a "No Entry" fence. It had powerful compulsions on it for humans to *stay away*, but allowed any denizens of the Underworld through without a problem.

Alexander pressed his face against the window, looking out over the beaches of Santa Monica eagerly.

"Do you want me to put the window down?"

"Yes, please!" He took deep breaths of the salty air. "What's that smell?"

"It's the ocean," Artemis replied, amused.

"What's an ocean?"

"It's a huge body of water that surrounds the continents."

"What's the continents?"

Artemis had to swallow down the overwhelming urge to giggle for no reason. She was happy to be with Alexander, to be teaching him something new. "A continent is a large land mass. Currently, we're on the North American continent."

"Why?"

"Why do you think?" Artemis turned the question around on him, refusing to fall into his trap.

"Because that's where we left home from?"

"That's right."

"Are we going to stay here?"

"Not permanently. What would Elati do without us?"

Alexander nodded solemnly at that. "And I'd miss Damien and Hestia and Maddie and Gus and Lee."

"But not Lyta and Atlanta?" Artemis asked, amused. "What about Luna?"

Alexander paused, head tilted to one

side as he considered the question. "Them too."

"Don't worry, we'll go home after this little adventure."

"Good." He opened his mouth and then closed it again.

Artemis met his eyes through the rearview mirror. "Ask."

"Where are we going?" Alexander blurted out.

"I'm impressed that you waited this long to ask me. We're going to the pier."

"What's a pier?"

This time Artemis did laugh. "It's usually a place where ships dock. This one is special."

"Why?"

"I think I'll let you find that out for yourself. We're almost there."

A few minutes later, Artemis was parking and helping Alexander out of the car. He stared at the pier.

"What is that?" he asked, pointing.

"There are rides of all sorts at this pier. Some, you'll be too little to go on. Others, we can go on together. There's also lots of food. I think we should start by getting some street dogs and then riding the carousel. What do you think?"

Alexander nodded vigorously. "Then can we go on the *big* wheel?"

"We'll check the height requirements, but I'm sure you'll be fine."

Alexander chose a green horse on the carousel, gripping the pole in front of him with both hands. He cheered each time the horse rose in the air.

"Did you want to learn how to ride a

real horse?" Artemis asked him afterward.

"I can't ride Lati?" he asked, looking disappointed.

"No, sweetheart. Her back isn't built to be ridden. But there's a stable with horses and ponies on the outskirts of Purgatory, and you can learn to ride one, if you want."

"Maybe."

"You don't have to decide right now," Artemis said. "And if you decide to try it and don't like it, you can stop immediately."

"Okay."

They got cotton candy before waiting in line for the ferris wheel. The pink and blue ball of spun sugar was almost bigger than Alexander's head.

Alexander gasped when the ferris wheel started moving, lifting them higher and higher in the air, letting them see far into the horizon. The wheel stopped with them at the top for a long time, and he held tightly to Artemis's hand.

"Are you okay?" she asked, concerned.

"I'm trying to do what Lee said," he replied. "But I can't make my fingers let go."

"What did Lee tell you to do?"

"He told me that when I feel scared, I should put my fingertips together until I'm calm. And then I'm supposed to look for something that's special. But Mom," his big gray eyes looked up at her, "I don't want to look around! It's too high!"

"That is really good advice," Artemis

said, liking Lee even more. "Why don't I hold your hands while you put your fingertips together? Let's start with that one, okay?"

Alexander had done it three times before the ferris wheel started again with a jerk, making him shriek.

Artemis held him firmly by the wrists. "The bar is in place. We're not going anywhere, okay?"

The trust in his eyes shook her to her core. "Next time, we should invite Lee. He can fly. Then if I fall, he can catch me."

"That's a good idea. Although, you know, I'm not completely helpless," Artemis said with a grin. The moon had risen, and although the sun was still low in the sky, she could still access her powers. She grabbed a thread of moonbeam, invisible to humans, but she could feel it, and fashioned it into a miniature staircase on the palm of her hand. She showed it to Alexander, who touched it gently with one finger. "If you fell, I would make a slide, much bigger than this, that would bring you down to the pier with a swish!"

"Swish!" Alexander repeated excitedly. "Can we do that?"

"It's for emergencies only. Using that much power would completely drain me. Your life is worth it. For fun, it is not." She booped his nose. "Do you understand?"

"Yes, Mom."

"So, I wanted to ask you..." she trailed off awkwardly.

Alexander looked up at her, confused.

"What's your favorite color?" she blurted out.

"Green! What's yours?" Alexander replied happily.

Artemis opened and closed her mouth a few times, not expecting the obvious question. "Pink, I guess."

"Pink like your lipstick!" Alexander said, reaching up and pressing one finger to her lips.

She kissed it and he pulled back, giggling. "What's your favorite thing to do at Maddie's?"

"I like to listen to stories that Hestia reads to us. And paint! And play outside."

Artemis waited a moment to see if he'd add anything else to the list. "What kind of stories?"

"Sometimes they're fairy stories, or princesses, or animals. I like the animal ones best. Do you like stories?"

"I do. I like the ones you tell me about your day."

"But those aren't stories," Alexander scoffed. "Those are real!"

"Stories about real life are called non-fiction, and they're still stories," Artemis said. "The made up ones are called fiction."

"Oh."

"Can you tell me more real life stories about Lee?" Artemis asked.

"He's a big dragon! He's blue. His wings are so so *so* big!" Alexander stretched his arms out to the side in an attempt to demonstrate. "He's silly and sometimes he pretends he's stuck in a handstand and can't get down. He doesn't always know how to play or how to do things that Maddie knows how to do, but Hestia teaches him the grown up things, and we teach him how to play."

"What do you mean, he doesn't know how to play?" Artemis asked.

"I gave him my train to play with me, and he didn't know that the trains could *talk*. He zoomed it around the rails." Alexander shook his head as if he were disgusted and Artemis chuckled.

"I'm sure he was happy that you showed him how to play properly."

"He said he didn't know how to play with them."

"Maybe he didn't have an awesome friend like you to show him," Artemis said, and smiled when he puffed up at her praise.

"I like it when he lets me sit beside him and puts his arm around me," Alexander confided. "He's so big, even when he's not a dragon. I feel safe."

"I'm glad you feel safe with him," Artemis replied. "I look forward to meeting him at your birthday party."

"Lee's coming to my birthday party?" Alexander asked excitedly.

"I've invited him."

"Can we go down to the beach?"

"Sure."

CHAPTER EIGHT

ON FRIDAY, FINLEY had to arrive at the daycare before any of the kids. He'd been helping out for a little over a week, and Maddie said she wanted to do a debrief with each of them—Augustine had done his the day before—to make sure they were getting on all right and didn't have any questions.

He didn't. Finley was actually surprised by how much he enjoyed his days at the daycare. Maybe it would be different if it was his job, because then he might have to stick to stricter rules, but this? This was working for him.

Even though he didn't really like kids.

But these four?

He'd do pretty much anything to protect them.

As he rolled out of bed and headed into the bathroom, he allowed himself a brief moment to think about Artemis, the single mother he'd hooked up with at the speed dating event.

Maybe I'd like her son?

He checked out his reflection in the mirror, and then shook his head. These kids were one thing.

A potential mate's kid?

He'd make a shit parent. It was better

to cut ties this way.

He still felt guilty for running so fast. She hadn't deserved that.

Not to mention he'd been as hard as a rock practically every minute he thought about her since. She'd been dressed prettily, not provocatively, her glasses giving her that school-teacher vibe. And then he'd undressed her—well, partially undressed her. The unexpectedness of her nipple piercings had almost made him come on the spot, like a teenager in his pants.

Her skin had been addictive; he'd wanted—no, *needed* to taste her. What had started out as a makeout session had quickly evolved into so much more.

Finley came back to the present to find himself leaning on the counter with one hand, the other unconsciously pulling on his cock. He rolled his eyes at himself and climbed in the shower, sighing as the hot water sluiced over his skin. He only got partway through soaping his body before his cock demanded attention again. "Fine," he muttered at it.

He closed his eyes again and Artemis immediately blossomed to life in his fantasy. She had been a wet dream come to life; he didn't even need to embellish in his memories.

He'd been the first person to eat her out. He couldn't believe that whoever had fathered her child hadn't wanted to go down on her. Her taste, the erotic sounds she'd made, the way she'd writhed against him... He'd remember them forever.

His fist sped up on his cock as he braced himself on the tile of the shower. The hot water hit the back of his neck and trickled down his body, heightening every sensation.

Finley wasn't sure when she'd started glowing. Before she'd told him she was about to come.

The burst of light when her orgasm hit had been blinding, both in intensity and beauty.

And she'd been as surprised as he had, which meant it hadn't happened before.

That thought brought him down from the edge a bit, so he pushed it aside and focused on what she'd looked like after, her skin glowing silver, her hair mussed, and her glasses slipping down her nose... Her shirt gaping open, exposing her perky breasts with those gleaming barbells piercing the tight little nipples... Her skirt rucked up and her pussy dripping her juices...

Finley's own orgasm caught him by surprise. He gasped, leaning against the wall as his release pulsed through him, legs shaking with the force.

I shouldn't be surprised. It's been like this every time.

Every single *damned* time he thought about her.

Finley shook himself out of the afterglow and finished his shower. He couldn't keep doing this, but he also couldn't stop thinking about her.

"That settles it," he muttered to

himself as he got dressed for the day. "First thing on Monday, I'll reach out to Aphrodite. See if she knows Artemis. And then I'll beg for forgiveness, on bended knee if I have to. Whatever it takes."

Mind made up, Finley ate without tasting it and left for the daycare. The sun had barely risen; the last wisps of fog still lingered in the air giving the Underworld a dream-like quality.

***

He looked up from his intense study of the desk in Maddie's office when she entered. She sat in the chair and pulled a piece of paper toward her.

"Any questions?"

"Not that I can think of," Finley

started, but then hesitated. "Are you sure I should come to the birthday party tomorrow?"

Maddie frowned, tilting her head to the side. "You were invited. Alexander loves you. Of course you should come."

"I don't know his parents at all. It feels weird going to a kid's birthday party without knowing them." Finley shifted awkwardly in the chair.

"Don't overthink it. Just be yourself," Maddie advised.

Finley chuckled. "I can't do both of those things. Pick one!"

Maddie offered him an understanding smile. "The most important thing is to be there for Alexander, right?"

"Right."

"Look..." Maddie crossed her arms as

best as she could over her pregnant belly. "Alexander's father is... Okay, you know how you think you're bad with kids?"

"Yeah." Finley squirmed internally.

"You're not, by the way. Trust me, I know kids. I've seen them with you. You're fantastic with them."

Finley blushed. He wasn't used to so much praise.

Maddie smiled sadly. "Anyway, this guy, he left Alexander's mom when she told him she was pregnant. Like, not cold feet, keep in touch, I need to process this big change. He full on left the Underworld and moved topside, never to be heard from or seen again." Maddie growled a little. "If I ever get my hands on that *bastard*— How can he *possibly* not want to be in Alexander's life? He's a fantastic kid! Everyone loves him."

She seethed quietly for a minute while Finley tried to figure out what to say, but she continued before he managed it.

"He was a con man, honestly. He only wanted money to gamble it away, and it didn't matter where he got the money from, always looking for the next big score. I don't know what she saw in him, but she was *way* too good for him."

"Sure sounds like it," Finley said, heart heavy for Alexander. Obviously his mom was doing a fantastic job raising him by herself, but sometimes a kid just wanted his dad. Heck, Finley himself was how old now, and he still wanted his dad sometimes.

Ask him if he could be a good potential dad even though he didn't know how one acted.

Well, they don't run away from a woman the instant she tells them that she has a kid, the unhelpful voice in his head supplied. Finley winced. He was *such* an asshole.

"Are you okay?" Maddie asked.

"I just..." Finley didn't want to spill all his problems out to her. She had enough on her plate. "I was thinking about how big a jerk I am."

"I'm sure you're not that bad," Maddie said with a chuckle.

"I ran away from a woman after eating... er, um... being *intimate* with her because she told me she has a son," he said flatly.

"Oh." Maddie covered her mouth with a hand. He had a sneaking suspicion she was trying not to laugh at him. "I'm sure you could apologize?" she suggested, her voice sounding choked.

"It was two weeks ago," Finley said, ashamed.

How had he let it go that long?

"Never underestimate a good apology," Maddie advised. "If you mean it and you have a good reason—and yes, being scared of kids is a pretty decent reason, especially if you can admit that you've had more experience with them now and you've realized you were mistaken—and you promise to make it up to her in some way..." The corners of her mouth twitched in amusement.

Finley caught her meaning and flushed.

Making it up to her on my knees was my plan, but I wasn't thinking that!

"I need to find her first. We didn't exchange information before I ran like a chicken."

"It shouldn't be too hard to find her. The Underworld is a lot like a small town in that way. Unless she was a human from the topside?"

"No, she was definitely a Goddess. Told me so herself." Finley resolutely pushed the image of her glowing in his arms out of his mind. "Her name is Artemis. I didn't get her last name, though."

"The Moon Goddess?" Maddie asked, her jaw dropping.

"That's the one." Finley shook his head and rubbed his face with his hands. "I haven't been able to get her out of my mind, you know? She's just... She's one of those women who are smart, funny, and sexy all in one package."

"Oh wow, a multi-dimensional woman. However did you find one of those?"

Finley looked up. "I know you're being sarcastic, and I don't appreciate your tone."

Maddie grinned. "Who, me?"

CHAPTER NINE

ON ALEXANDER'S BIRTHDAY, Artemis always felt the urge to wake him up at 12:34 in the morning, the exact time of his birth. He'd arrived at that auspicious time of the night, just as the moon rose in the sky, its beams shining into her window.

She'd never forget that moment.

The pain of childbirth was long forgotten, but the feeling of the moonbeams caressing her distended belly in time with her last contraction... And then the pressure had been gone and a healthy scream had pierced the night.

Artemis had insisted on the baby being given to her immediately unless medically necessary, and her beautiful little boy had been placed directly in the light of the moon on her belly. She could practically hear the contentment from both the baby and the moon.

It had been magical.

But she wasn't about to wake a three year old from a deep sleep in order to recount his birth story. Maybe when he was a teenager. She paled at the thought.

Her baby, all grown up?

What would his personality be like?

Would he still like to lean against her while they sat in the backyard, or would that be too babyish for him?

Artemis got out of bed and padded across the hall to Alexander's room, pushing open the door as quietly as possible.

He was asleep on his back, completely uncovered. His belly was poking out between his pajama top and pants. The moonlight shone over him, covering him like a blanket.

She put a hand over her heart and tiptoed in to pull the sheet and blanket up.

Alexander hummed in his sleep and rolled onto his side, reaching out for his stuffed teddy bear with eyes still firmly closed.

Artemis scooped the bear off the floor and put it within reach, amusement twitching her lips when Alexander found it and pulled it tightly against his small body.

"May you keep your loving nature," Artemis mouthed the words and pressed a kiss to sleep-tousled hair. He smiled a little and squeezed his bear tighter.

Artemis left the room, closing the door behind her silently. Back in her bed, she fell into a deep sleep the instant her head touched her pillow.

***

She woke the next morning to a warm little body climbing into her bed.

Alexander wormed his way under her

arm and turned so his back was pressed against her front, hugging her hand. "Good morning," she whispered into blond curls. "Happy birthday, little one."

Alexander gave a happy wiggle. "I'm three!" he announced proudly. "One, two, three!" He held up fingers as he counted. "Three."

"Very good, sweetheart." She snuggled him close. "What do you want for breakfast?"

"I want to eat in the garden!"

Artemis chuckled. "I didn't ask *where*, I asked *what*."

"Ohhhhh!" Alexander drew the sound out until Artemis tickled his ribs, making him shriek with laughter. When things calmed back down, he said, "Pancakes, please."

"Pancakes! What? My son wants pancakes? I'm shocked. This is my shocked face," Artemis deadpanned.

Alexander twisted in her arms to look at her face. "It looks like your regular face."

"That's my point." She smiled down at him. "I know you love pancakes."

"Can they please have blueberries in them?"

"Of course." Artemis stretched lazily. "I guess we should get up, shouldn't we?"

"Yes!" Alexander immediately bounced up onto his knees.

"You have entirely too much energy for this time of the morning," Artemis complained.

Alexander jumped on the bed twice

before falling onto his bum. "Luna says I have the right amount of energy for a kid."

Artemis laughed. "She's right, as usual."

They got out of bed and toddled into the kitchen in their pajamas, mostly because Artemis didn't want to bathe Alexander twice before they left for the party.

By the time the first batch of pancakes was cooking in the buttered frying pan, Alexander was covered in flour from head to toe.

"How did you manage this?" Artemis asked him with a shake of her head. "You look good enough to eat!" She made munching noises as she scooped him up in her arms, getting flour all over herself as well.

Alexander shrieked with laughter and wrapped his arms around her neck. "I don't know."

"Of course you don't, my little monkey."

"Mom?"

"Yes, darling?"

"How are we going to get the flour out of our hair?"

"Let me flip these pancakes and then we're going to do a little experiment." Pancakes flipped and cooking on the second side, Artemis sat Alexander on the counter beside the sink. "Let's see what happens to the flour when we wash our hands." The white powder washed off easily under the water.

"Will that happen with our hair too?"

Alexander asked excitedly.

"I'm worried it might clump," Artemis said, drying her hands on the cloth.

"I can shake it off!" Alexander shook his head like a dog, flour flying everywhere.

Artemis tried to stop him before it was too late and then sighed in resignation. "I was thinking more of using the vacuum."

"On me?" Alexander stared, wide-eyed.

"On you, me, and the entire kitchen!" Artemis replied dramatically.

"Wow! Vacuum me, Mom!" He stood still with his arms outstretched.

"Just a minute, I need to pull these off." Pancakes saved on a platter, and a new batch put on the stove, Artemis retrieved the vacuum and turned it on her son. He wiggled and giggled under the suction. It didn't get everything, but it got most of it, at least. Then she turned her attention to herself. The kitchen would have to wait until the pancakes were off the burner and kept warm in the oven.

Finally, she turned off the stove and started to clean up.

"Get the broom and sweep everything on the floor into a little pile on the X tile, please," Artemis asked Alexander.

"Yes, Mom!"

She watched him out of the corner of her eye. He loved to help so much that she'd bought him a child-sized broom. Using painter's tape, she'd marked a large X on the tile closest to the under-cabinet suction, and he was always happy to help her with the chore.

She cleaned off the counters and stove using a wet cloth, and got the widely dispersed flour with the vacuum. By the time she was done, so was Alexander.

"Can I push the button, Mom? Please?"

Artemis pretended to hesitate. "Well, I don't know..."

"It's my birthday! Please, Mom?"

"Sure you can." She lifted him up onto the counter so he could reach the switch that turned on the suction, and then put him back down so that he could use his broom to sweep the dirt closer to the opening. When it was all gone, she said, "Oh no! Don't let your toes get taken! Noooo!!"

Alexander giggled. "My toes are fine, Mom. See? Can I turn it off?"

Artemis picked him up again to flick the switch. Then she made a big show of checking his feet, counting all his toes and pretending to miss one. "Only nine! Oh no! What should we do? I'll call Hera, maybe she can grow it back!"

"It's there, look! See, Mom?" Alexander wiggled his toes and pulled them up so that he could count them too. "Ten!"

"Oh, thank goodness!" Artemis gasped, hand to her chest. "I really didn't know how to fix that!"

"You're funny, Mom." Alexander gave her a tight squeeze around her neck. "Can we eat now?"

"Have some blueberries. We both need to get clean," Artemis said. "Actually, why don't we take the bowl with us? Then you can eat them in the bath."

"I can *do* that?" Alexander asked incredulously.

Artemis laughed. "Yes, of course. Not every day, and not with crumbly things. Can you imagine trying to get clean and there are cookie crumbs in the bath with you?"

"It would be messy."

"Quite," Artemis agreed solemnly. "Come on then." She picked up the bowl and held out her hand for him.

***

After Alexander's bath and a shower for

her, they got dressed and took their breakfast out onto the patio. Elati greeted them with a squeak, prancing across the yard.

"Lati is happy to see us, Mom!" Alexander exclaimed. "Can I share my pancake with her?"

"That is so thoughtful, sweetheart. Why don't we give her one all on her own, rather than you sharing yours?" Artemis suggested.

"She needs a plate!" Alexander said reproachfully when Artemis placed a pancake on the clover nearest to them.

"Watch her."

Elati eagerly trotted over to them and delicately nibbled on the edge of the golden brown pastry. Her long tongue licked over the entire thing and then she moved back to the edge, taking small bites and chewing.

"It's better that she doesn't have a plate because she might try to bite it by accident," Artemis explained to her avid son. "If she takes a bite of clover, it won't hurt her. Look how she's claimed the whole thing by licking it. Aren't you glad that you aren't sharing yours?"

Alexander shrugged his shoulders and picked up his pancake with both hands. "I don't mind."

Artemis laughed. "Better you than me. *I* wouldn't want to share deer slobber."

"*Mom*! Lati might *hear* you!" Alexander shushed her.

"I don't think she'll take offense, darling. Deer don't think about these things the same way we do." Artemis stabbed the last bite of her pancake with her fork. "Are you ready for your party?"

Alexander stuffed the rest of his pancake in his mouth and grinned at her, nodding enthusiastically.

"Thank you for not attempting to speak with your mouth *that* full," Artemis said with a shake of her head. "Chew, swallow, and *then* we can leave."

They brushed their teeth and then walked over to the daycare. Balloons, tied to a stick stuck in the ground in front of the gate to the backyard, bounced in the breeze.

"Pretty!" Alexander exclaimed. "Can I have one?"

"Maybe later, on the way home," Artemis replied. "Right now, they're directing people to your party."

"Okay." Alexander seemed perfectly happy with that reasoning and ran through the gate to join the party. He came to an abrupt stop just beyond the wall of the building and stared wide-eyed at the backyard.

Artemis followed more sedately. She came up behind him and put a hand on his shoulder. The backyard was a sight to behold. "Pretty incredible, isn't it?"

There were balloons tied to the fence at intervals, and an enormous drawing of an elephant on the wall. In the large grassy space sat an inflatable climbing gym decorated with a giraffe, a lion, and a monkey.

"Mom!" Alexander gasped. "Do you see?"

"I see a lot of things," Artemis replied, amused.

"The cake looks like Lati!"

Artemis looked past the brightly-colored decor to the food table near the back door of the daycare. The cake was a simple rectangle, but it was designed to look like a meadow, complete with delicate spun-sugar flowers on top. Topping the cake was a toy version of Elati. "She's not made of cake. She's a toy for you to play with."

"Ohh. Good." Alexander looked relieved. "I wanted to eat cake, but I didn't want to eat Lati."

"Even if she had been cake, you wouldn't actually be eating her, you know that right?"

Alexander frowned at her. "I know,

Mom."

"Are you a threenager already?" Artemis asked, half-anxious.

"I'm *three*."

"Go play, sweetheart."

Alexander immediately raced for the inflatable climbing wall and clambered up it with ease. At the top, he shouted with joy before swishing down the slide.

Artemis joined Maddie, Hera, and Demi at the food table. "This looks amazing. Alexander is thrilled." She caught sight of a brightly-colored piñata in the shape of a horse hanging from the support beam of the play structure. "Thank you."

Demi smiled. "This is what I do. I'm happy you're happy."

Artemis had the overwhelming urge

to continue the praise and was grateful when the first party guests arrived. For a while, she was kept busy greeting the parents of the other kids at the daycare. She knew most of them fairly well, but it was still a little nerve-wracking to shake the hand of and make small talk with Lucifer himself, the Lord of the Underworld. His daughter, Atlanta, had only been attending the daycare for about nine months or so.

Jaden and his brothers were the last to arrive. The children instantly swarmed the three large men, a testament to how much the kids loved them. Artemis watched, amused, as the kids were tossed gently from one to another, shrieks of glee filling the air.

"They were a good choice for helping

you out," Artemis overheard Hestia tell Maddie. "The McKellen brothers may look intimidating, but they're marshmallows with the kids. Look at Finley with Alexander. You'd never know that he was terrified of kids a few short weeks ago."

Finley?

No, it couldn't be.

Artemis focused on the men across the backyard. There was Augustine, Hera's mate, playing with little Atlanta and Lyta. Jaden had Damien on his shoulders. And... The third man turned to face her, Alexander upside down in his arms. Her stomach swooped.

It *was* Finley.

He filled out a navy blue polo shirt as if he'd been poured into it, his biceps bulging as he cradled the little boy.

Her heart beat faster. Her hands grew clammy. All of a sudden, she wondered if she'd remembered to brush her hair after her shower that morning and quickly ran her hand over her head, only to find that she'd tied it up in a messy topknot.

Maybe he won't notice me!

She wildly fought the urge to hide underneath the tablecloth covering the snack table.

But Finley's blue eyes had locked onto her and he was walking purposefully toward her, putting Alexander gently down on the ground once he reached her. He opened his mouth, but Artemis beat him to it.

"I thought you didn't like kids?" she

asked before mentally kicking herself.

She wanted him to ask her out, didn't she?

But Finley smiled. "I thought I didn't. I still don't particularly like kids in general, but I very much like these four. It's been a steep learning curve these past few weeks, but Alexander's been on hand to teach me the ropes. Which kid is yours?" He ruffled Alexander's hair when he mentioned him, making the boy smile up at him.

Before Artemis could reply, Alexander said, "Mom, this is Lee! He's the blue dragon I told you about."

The shock of realization hit both adults at once. Artemis could tell by the widening of Finley's eyes, even as she was overwhelmed by the fact that not only had she been hearing all about Lee for weeks, but he'd saved her son from being kidnapped twice.

"Umm, hi?" she said hesitantly.

CHAPTER TEN

ALL FINLEY COULD think was *Maddie knew this would happen.*

She knew Artemis was Alexander's mom. And she didn't warn me.

A quick glance at Maddie showed her smirking at him, obviously pleased that he had been caught off-balance.

His gaze dropped back down to Artemis's turned up face. She looked just as surprised as he felt. She looked gorgeous, in a different way than she had at the speed dating event. There, she'd been dressed seductively. Here, she was wearing a casual cream-colored sweater that slipped off one shoulder and a pair of black leggings that looked sculpted to her ass.

"You look amazing," he said, his tongue trying to trip him up on those simple words.

"So do you." Her gaze skittered over his chest and arms before she pushed her glasses up her nose slightly, adjusting them with a practiced hand. "So you're the Lee that Alexander hasn't stopped talking about. I need to thank you for what you've done."

His mind jumped to all the ways she could thank him, including but not limited to letting him strip her clothing from her and feast on her juices once more. Pulling his thoughts away from her beautiful body with a strength of will he wouldn't have had if they'd been alone, he cleared his throat. "I would never stand by."

Looking horrified, Artemis brought one hand to her mouth. "I didn't think you would! I meant that I'm glad you were there. Thank you."

Finley shifted from one foot to the other. "Not a problem. I'm glad I was there too."

God, could he get any more awkward?

"I didn't know Alexander was your son."

"I didn't know you were Lee. What a pair we are!" Her chuckle sounded forced.

"Look, I owe you an apology," Finley said. "I shouldn't have left right after we—" He cut himself off, suddenly aware that the other adults were all listening in on their conversation. "—met," he finished weakly. "I couldn't get you out of my mind. That was a huge mistake, and I'd really like the chance to try again."

Artemis crossed her arms. "You left because I told you I had a child. That's a pretty big 'mistake' to forgive. Not to mention that you left when I was still vulnerable. It's been two weeks. What makes you think you can apologize and I'll take you back *now*? How have things changed so drastically in two weeks?"

"Fair enough." Finley rubbed his

chin, trying to formulate the proper phrasing. "When we met, I had just had my orientation meeting here. Damien had painted on a wall. It was... a lot. I was scared of what the idea of dating a single mother would entail, and honestly, I panicked. I like to be prepared. I like to know all the facts in advance. Kids are hard to prepare for. I should have stuck around and talked to you about how I was feeling. I regret my actions. As for what changed..."

Finley waved a hand around himself, encompassing the kids and the daycare. "I've been here multiple days since then. Hestia has been a rock. And the kids have taught me a lot. I'm still a little anxious, but being around them has shown me that they're pretty cool kids.

And yesterday, I asked Maddie if she knew who you were, that I wanted to try to find you, explain myself, and beg you to try again with me." He spread his arms wide. "She didn't tell me you were Alexander's mom. But this is me, explaining and hoping to get a second chance."

Artemis bit her lip as she stared at him. "I'm going to have to think about it."

His heart sank to his toes. "Okay," he whispered. He turned away, heading for the gate. He passed Jaden on the way. "I'm going for a walk to clear my head. Be back in a bit." He didn't wait for his brother's answer before he pushed through the gate, pausing only to hear the lock click into place behind him.

Did I seriously just lay everything in my heart out in front of all those people?

The parents of the kids I help look after?

And all she said in return was that she'll think about it?

Finley started walking along the sidewalk, not really paying attention to where his feet were taking him.

What the hell am I supposed to do now?

The obvious answer, "wait and see what her decision is," was an unpleasant pill to swallow, even worse than the thought that he had to return to the party. It was Alexander's birthday party, and he didn't deserve to have it ruined by Finley being too embarrassed to go back.

Sighing, Finley abruptly turned around, heading back the way he had come. A car zipped past him and he scowled. There was no way they were obeying the speed limit in the area.

When he returned to the daycare, he reached through the bars to unlock the gate, ready to apologize again, but this time to Alexander for leaving so unexpectedly. Finley scanned the busy backyard, looking for the head of blond curls. Not finding him, he frowned.

Maybe he's inside?

Avoiding Artemis, he went instead to Maddie, who was standing near the inflatable climbing gym. "Hey, where's Alexander? Is he inside?"

"I don't think so. I'm afraid you'll have to ask Artemis where he is,"

Maddie teased.

Finley groaned quietly. "Do I have to?"

"If you want to know where Alexander is, yes."

"Fine." Finley sucked up his courage and made his way over to the last person he wanted to talk to right now. "Is Alexander inside?" he asked sheepishly, not wanting to look at her.

"I thought he was with you." She sounded pissed.

"*What*?" Finley's gaze snapped up from the ground to meet hers. "I would *never* take a kid away from anywhere without asking their parent's permission first. Where is he?"

Artemis's anger dropped instantly, replaced by panic. "I don't know. I noticed he was gone when you left, and I just assumed... Did you lock the gate behind you?"

"I did. And it was still locked when I returned. Have you checked inside?"

"No."

"I'll do that now. You look around out here and then meet me inside. There are lots of hidey holes."

Heart pounding, Finley burst through the door into the daycare. Nothing looked out of place. He started with the obvious places that he'd seen the children use for hide and seek, checking the bathrooms and rooms down the hallway, calling Alexander's name as he moved through the building. There was no sign of him anywhere.

Artemis was waiting for him in the

dining space when he got back from the sleeping room, pacing frantically. "They've got him. Whoever has been trying to kidnap him, they got him!" she cried. "How did they manage to grab him out of a party filled with adults?"

Finley was grim. "We need to tell the others. Start a search. Maybe he climbed the gate and is wandering the neighborhood."

"He is a good climber," Artemis acknowledged. "But he'd also know not to leave without telling me. And *why* would he leave? His friends are here! I'm here! There's food here!"

"Maybe he wanted to follow me. I don't know. Come on." Finley opened the back door and followed her outside.

"Did you two make up?" Jaden asked

slyly.

"Alexander is missing," Artemis said quietly, almost as if she didn't want to believe he might have been kidnapped. "I—" She broke off with a gasping sob that wrenched Finley's heart.

Chloe stepped forward, taking charge of the situation. "We need to arrange a search. Augustine, Jaden, Finley, you three are aerial support. Fly over the neighborhood in a spiral, starting close by and spreading out. Check in here every fifteen minutes. Be thorough. Go."

Finley leapt into the air and transformed while Chloe started giving more jobs to the others; Maddie and Hestia were to look after the kids, the other parents were to search the grounds and daycare extensively.

Artemis looked small and pale. All Finley wanted to do was reassure her that Alexander was all right, that he would be found and returned safely.

But he couldn't. He could feel it in his bones. Alexander had been kidnapped, and they had no leads.

The only good thing about this search is that it's still morning and there's good light. If he is walking around, we'll be able to see him.

When fifteen minutes were up, he made a mental note of where he was and returned to the daycare, followed closely by his brothers.

Maddie greeted them in the backyard, a grim expression on her face. "He's nowhere in the daycare, grounds or building," she said once they'd shifted back into human form. "Chloe gave everyone a section of the neighborhood to search on foot, but I agree with Artemis; this is probably a kidnapping."

Finley's jaw clenched tightly. "No sign from the air." His brothers echoed him. "Shall we go back out?"

"Yes, Chloe said another fifteen minute scan and then come back again."

"Okay." Finley turned away to jump into the air when the snack table caught his eye. "What—" He walked closer to the cake and felt his heart drop. Any chance that Alexander had wandered away on his own was gone with the sight of the knife stabbed into the cake. Pinned to the cake by the blade was a note, the letters cut from a magazine like an 80's movie ransom note.

Want to see your son again?

Stay close to the phone.

We'll call with details.

"What kind of sick *fucks* would do this?" Finley whispered, drawing the attention of the others.

Maddie let out a quiet scream and Jaden was instantly at her side, supporting her.

Augustine was pale with fury. He moved around the snack table to the various paraphernalia that Demi and Hera had brought with them, searching through boxes for what he was looking for. Finally he growled, "Go get baby powder from the change station, and a paintbrush from the art area. Clean and dry it thoroughly."

Finley rushed to do as he was asked.

There was a chance that there were fingerprints on the knife handle. Once he'd followed Augustine's instructions, he returned to the backyard, trailed by the ever-curious Damien.

The cake had been covered by a box.

"I got a little eager," Augustine said sheepishly. "I was going to dust for fingerprints myself, but after thinking about it while you were inside, I realized that if I messed up, I would ruin any prints that were found. Besides, this is Demi's knife that she brought for cutting the cake, so there will be more prints than just hers."

"So we covered it up to protect it and figured we could get everything ready and then Chloe could try dusting for prints," Jaden supplied.

"When will Chloe be back?" Finley asked.

"A few minutes," Maddie replied.

Finley spent those few minutes debating with himself on whether he should go inside and help look after the kids but be near Artemis, or stay outside. He paced back and forth between the door and the inflatable climbing gym, one eye on Damien as he played on the balloon-like structure.

He heard people returning before he saw them, low anxious voices filtering in on the breeze as they walked up the space beside the building to the gate.

Chloe was first. Something in the brothers' faces must have given away that there was bad news because she turned to Damien and said cheerfully,

"Why don't you go inside and show your parents your art projects?"

"Okay."

Once he was out of earshot, she asked, "What is it? Did you find him?"

Augustine removed the box off the cake. "This is almost worse," he admitted. "We have not touched it, but we got everything for you to dust for prints."

Chloe chuckled. "I think I'll leave that for the forensic team. I'm not trained in that."

"That's my knife," Demi said hesitantly.

"Then we'll need your prints too, so we can eliminate them easily," Chloe reassured her. "Let's pack that up as evidence and take it to the station. You'll come with me, Demi."

"I'm going to see if I can find the kidnappers," Finley announced to nobody in particular.

Chloe put her hand on his arm and he had the urge to shake her off, but all she said was, "Keep checking in every fifteen minutes," which he appreciated. He had to do *something*, and waiting in the backyard was killing him.

He nodded abruptly and took off into the air, hoping to find a clue, a hint of Alexander somewhere... anywhere. He thought perhaps Alexander had been taken in a car, so he'd be further away when he was moved. Finley stretched his hearing to its limits, but even he couldn't hear across Purgatory.

And what if the little boy had been

taken topside?

That thought made him pause for a moment, hovering in midair.

Didn't the portals to topside record the person who passed through?

In which case, they'd know whether they needed to expand their search. He made a mental note to mention that possibility to Chloe when he returned next time and continued on his search. She would know how to get that information from the various portals scattered throughout the Underworld.

A car... Finley frowned—a scary thing to see on a dragon—and wondered why that was ringing a bell. Probably due to the black sedan and the man with the snake tattoo on his hand that had tried to kidnap Alexander a couple weeks ago.

His innate sense of time tingled; he'd been in the air for fifteen minutes and he needed to return.

Maybe they've found a clue.

CHAPTER ELEVEN

ARTEMIS WAS PANICKING. All her power, and there was not a thing she could do. Alexander was probably scared and wanting her and...

She couldn't think like that.

Swallowing down the lump in her throat, she focused on the game she was playing with Atlanta involving all the stuffed animals in the daycare and the play tea set. Every time Artemis put something down, Atlanta would frown and say, "No, not there. *Here!*"

She really needs to learn the power of the "yes, and", Artemis thought, amused in spite of herself.

Finley dashed into the daycare from the back yard, and Artemis's heart leapt in hope, but he didn't say anything to her, only grabbing a paintbrush from the easel before cleaning it vigorously at the sink. Seemingly satisfied, he then dried it, grabbed the baby powder from the change table, and ran out the door again, Damien following behind.

When Artemis moved to retrieve the boy, Hestia shook her head. "Maddie's out there. Damien's safe. She'll keep an eye on him."

Biting back the retort that Alexander

had vanished while *everyone* had been outside, Artemis resettled herself on the floor. "Would you like me to read you a book, Atlanta?"

"No. Play tea party," the little girl replied, continuing her placement of the tea cups and toys meant to be cookies.

Artemis shrugged her shoulders and held in a sigh. "Whatever you want."

Halfway through the interminable tea party, in which Artemis wasn't one hundred percent sure what was going on half the time, the rest of the adults returned to the backyard. From what she could see through the back door, they didn't have any news for her. She slumped back against the leg of the couch, feeling defeated.

Damien burst in through the door,

followed by his parents, and led them around the room, showing them all the art he'd made recently that he hadn't brought home yet.

His boisterousness cut into her heart and Artemis got to her feet, hurrying out of the room. The hallway led her to a quiet room where four cots were tucked away and a plush rocking chair was in the center of the room. She took off her glasses, holding them loosely in one hand, and sank into it with a stifled cry. Drawing her knees up, she pressed her face against her thighs. Only then did she let her tears flow. All her anxiety, her worry for Alexander, her panic... She let them all out through her sobs. At the end, she felt calmer, but shaky.

"What was it that Alexander said Lee,

no, *Finley*, taught him?" she whispered to herself. "Put my fingers together until I'm calm, and then find one special thing to look at." Artemis pressed her fingers together, one at a time, taking deep breaths with each fingertip that touched. To her surprise, she did feel better afterward. Then she looked around the room for something special about it. The room was pretty sparse, but then she spotted a leftover blue blanket on one of the cots. It wasn't folded; thrown haphazardly over the cot as if tossed there by a child, which was probably the case.

Feeling more under control, Artemis got up and left the room. The knees of her leggings were wet, making her pants stick awkwardly to her skin.

All the kids were gone, taken home by their parents. Maddie was washing dishes with Hestia, and Finley was talking quietly into his phone as he paced back and forth in the living room.

"What's going on?" Artemis asked the women at the sink, picking up a dishtowel.

"Chloe took Demi to the police station to get her fingerprints," Maddie said.

"*What?*" Artemis gasped. "She would never have anything to do with this!"

The other women frowned, confused.

"You weren't there!" Maddie exclaimed. "I am so sorry! No, of course she didn't. But her cake knife was used to stab the ransom note into the cake. They want to be able to eliminate her prints easily."

Artemis's ears were buzzing. "Ransom note?" she said weakly.

Maddie pinched her lips shut, eyes wide and apologetic. "I'm so sorry!"

Hestia put a hand on her arm. "Chloe is taking care of it. They said they would contact you. The instant they do, let Chloe know."

"So he didn't run away? He *was* taken?" Artemis felt a sense of relief knowing even that much. "*How*?"

"We have no idea. I'm so sor—" Maddie cut herself off from apologizing again. "Whatever you need, we're here for you."

"Thanks." Artemis offered a small smile. "Who is Finley talking to?"

"Chloe, I think. He had the idea to check the portal logs to topside. Whether

Alexander was registered passing through them or not, we'll have a better idea of where to look for him," Hestia replied.

"That's a great idea," Artemis said, surprised. "And if he's still in the Underworld, what? Will we go door to door and ask if they've seen a little blond boy?"

"We'll figure it out. Let Chloe do her job," Hestia advised.

Finley closed his phone with a snap and slipped it into his pocket. He fixed Artemis with his dark blue eyes. "Chloe says that no portals have been pinged. Alexander is still in the Underworld."

A sense of profound relief filled Artemis, making her knees buckle. Finley caught her the instant she started to sway, his masculine scent filling her nostrils and better than any smelling salts at clearing her head. She took deep breaths in through her nose, enthralled by the way he enveloped her, his arms banded around her waist, supporting her. But she couldn't stay like this forever, unfortunately. She stabilized and nodded at him. He released her immediately; the only hint that he was reluctant to do so was the way his fingers dragged along her arms long after he released her.

She met Maddie and Hestia's knowing smirks and willed the flush out of her cheeks, focusing on Finley again. "Does she say what to do next?"

"Hm? Oh, Chloe." The big man shook his head slightly.

Was he as distracted by her presence as she was by his?

"She says to go home and keep your phone nearby. Everyone at the station is working overtime on this, trying to find him. Once you get the call, notify her immediately."

Artemis swallowed hard.

Go home?

Without Alexander?

She didn't know if she could bear it.

Something in her expression must have given her away, because Finley added, "You can stay with my brothers and I, if you want. Give you a taste of what it's like to have messy, loud boys in your house."

His joke fell flat, but Artemis appreciated that he was attempting to lift her spirits. "Yes, please. I don't think I could survive the empty house."

"Not a problem. Shall we?" Finley offered her his arm.

She said goodbye, complete with hugs for the two women, and then tucked her hand over his. "Oh my gosh, I need to tell Luna! She was supposed to be here, but she didn't make it on time. I hope everything's all ght!"

Luna answered on the second ring. "I'm so sorry I'm late, Artemis! I'll be there in half an hour, I promise. Save me a slice of cake?"

Artemis told her the whole story, and was very proud of herself for her voice only wobbling a little.

Luna was devastated. "If I'd been there, I might have seen something! I'm so sorry, Artemis!"

"It's okay. There's no guarantee that it would have gone any differently if you had been here." Artemis sniffed and took the tissue that Finley held out for her. "I won't be in the office until this is resolved. Please arrange my appointments accordingly on Monday morning. I'll keep you posted, okay?"

"Yes. Yes, of course. Whatever you need," Luna said. "I hope you get him back before then, though. Do you want me to come over? Do you want to come to my place?"

"No, no, I'm going to Lee's." Artemis used the name Alexander had been calling Finley because she'd been talking about him to Luna for the past couple weeks. Did she ever have a lot to fill

Luna in on once she got back to the office! Artemis couldn't find the optimism inside herself to agree with Luna's hopes. Maybe if they knew who had taken him... but they didn't. "I'll be keeping my phone handy. Call if there's an emergency." They hung up.

Finley nodded at her. "Ready to go?"

"Yes. Sorry for the delay."

"No worries. We've got time." Finley opened the front door for her before stopping suddenly.

There was a man in uniform with his finger raised to push the doorbell. "Good afternoon. Medusa, I presume?" he said, looking at Artemis.

"No. Maddie?" Artemis called over her shoulder into the kitchen and then made room for her to talk to the cop.

"How can I help you?" Maddie asked, supporting her belly protectively with one hand and leaning on the doorframe with the other.

The cop handed her a business card. "I just wanted to make sure you had the correct number for the mother of the kidnapped child. She's been told to call us immediately once they've contacted her, right?"

"I think you should be talking to the mother herself," Maddie said, handing Artemis the card.

Artemis barely glanced at it. "Yes, I make note of all the pertinent details and then call right away."

The man nodded and ruffled a hand through his hair. Her eyes were drawn to where his sleeve rode up, exposing a snake tattoo on his hand that continued under his sleeve. "They'll probably demand money. Get it together as quickly as you can to pay them. The most important thing is for you to get your son back safely."

"I can earn more money. I can't survive without my son," Artemis said.

"Right. Do you have any idea who could have done this? Any enemies? Anyone who has threatened you lately?" The cop pulled out his phone and looked up at her expectantly.

"Well..." Artemis trailed off, uneasy. The cop raised his eyebrow questioningly. "I did have a verbal altercation with Mercury at the office recently. He was the reason I was late to pick up my son when the first failed attempt at kidnapping occurred."

"Good to know." The cop tapped on his phone, writing the information down. "We've been hearing shady rumors about that guy for a while. He's bad news. Definitely someone to look into." He snapped his phone closed and slid it into his pocket. "Do keep in touch." He tapped the card she was still holding in limp fingers. "We'll do everything we can to get your son back to you safe and sound." He gave a small salute before turning and walking down the front walk.

Artemis sagged a little and Finley caught her by the elbow, strong and sure by her side.

"Let's get you somewhere a little more comfortable," Finley suggested.

"Somewhere that isn't full of memories and you can just be you."

"Okay," she whispered in reply.

They left without further fanfare, walking the short distance to Finley's house.

Artemis wasn't sure what she'd expected to see when they arrived. It was a bachelor pad for three very large, in both forms, dragon shifters. The cute little two-storey house with a white picket fence surprised her. "You live here?" she asked.

"Yup, we have ever since we moved to Purgatory," Finley said, holding the gate open for her. "It's close enough to the surrounding forests that we could easily go there to stretch our wings, back before we felt comfortable shifting in public. Dragon shifters had a bad rap back when we were put to sleep, and we didn't really know what to expect when we woke up. So we moved around topside, never staying in one place for too long, until we heard about Purgatory, and then we came here."

"I'm glad you did," Artemis said shyly. She pushed her glasses up her nose as she walked up the pathway to the door. "Alexander talks about you all the time, you know. More than Gus, who I assume is Augustine?"

Finley chuckled. "I call him Auggie sometimes, to get on his nerves. Yes, the kids call him Gus. I'm actually surprised by how much I'm enjoying my time at the daycare. I wouldn't have volunteered if it hadn't been for Jaden and his mate, but it has been an enriching experience."

"I know what you mean," Artemis confided. "I didn't want kids, you know. I was terrified that I would be a horrible mother. I almost had an abortion."

Finley stayed quiet, unlocking and opening the front door for her.

"I didn't, obviously. I... Oh, this sounds silly when I say it out loud." Artemis flushed, turning away from Finley's riveted expression to look around the cozy living room.

"Nothing you've said is silly. It's something that is important to you, and I am willing to listen if you are willing to tell me."

"I asked the moon what I should do," Artemis whispered. She sank onto one of the couches, practically being enveloped by the plushness of it.

"That makes sense, you being the Moon Goddess," Finley said when she didn't continue, sitting beside her on the couch. "What did the moon say?"

"The moon doesn't really *talk*, exactly. It's more like feelings. It feels content, or sad, or angry." Artemis rubbed her hands on the knees of her leggings. They were still wet; she'd forgotten about that and wrinkled her nose at the unpleasant feeling.

"I went out into my backyard the night I found out I was pregnant, and I asked the moon what I should do. The feeling of warmth, of love, that I felt from the moon for my barely conceived child was overwhelming." She smiled, remembering the sensation. "I knew I had to keep the baby." Her smile wobbled. "And now he's—" She cut off, unable to continue.

"Come here," Finley murmured, wrapping an arm around her shoulders when she followed his instructions.

His warmth and strength surrounding her once more, Artemis let her tears go, sobbing into his chest until she had nothing left. Exhausted, she let the darkness take her.

CHAPTER TWELVE

FINLEY'S HEART WAS breaking for the beautiful woman asleep in his arms. The person she loved most in the world was missing, and there was absolutely nothing that anyone could do until the kidnappers either called or made a mistake.

God, Goddess, whatever deities existed that could grant his plea, he hoped the kidnappers made a mistake.

He looked down at the Goddess sleeping. She seemed younger, more at peace. Her glasses were slipping down her nose, so he carefully removed them with his free hand and placed them on the side table next to the couch. He could just barely reach it, but had to stretch.

Artemis whimpered in her sleep, an adorable furrow appearing on her brow, until he cuddled her close again and she burrowed deeper against his chest.

The movement shifted her sweater further off her shoulder, dropping down her arm and revealing the creamy white skin of the top of her breast. A hint of the pink of her areola was visible at the edge of the neckline and his mouth watered. He loved women that went without a bra. Even better when he couldn't tell through the clothing that she was naked underneath, and then the shirt slipped off the shoulder to reveal no strap.

So sexy.

Finley averted his eyes, not wanting to get aroused. She didn't need him pawing at her when she was so torn up about her son.

"Did you take my glasses off?" she asked, her voice slurred by sleep.

"Yes. Sorry. They were falling off."

"That's okay." She curled against him more and the sweater's neckline slipped further, exposing the edge of her dusky pink nipple with the silver barbell through it.

"Artemis," Finley ground out through

clenched teeth.

"What?" She blinked up at him innocently.

He blew out a long breath. "Either fix your shirt so that I can't see down it or take it off," he growled.

"Oh!" Artemis glanced down at herself.

He waited patiently for her to make up her mind, not wanting to push her one way or the other.

"I don't think I'm up for sex," she said at last.

"That's totally fi—" Finley cut himself off when she sat up and whipped her sweater off over her head. His fantasies, his memories, had not done her justice. He drank in the sight of her as she swung her leg across his, settling herself in his lap. "Even more stunning than I remember," he murmured. "Can I touch you?"

"Not yet," she replied, a coy smile playing at her lips. She ran her hands up her belly and over her ribs. Instead of cupping her breasts the way that Finley would have, she trailed her fingertips up her sternum, bypassing them completely.

Finley groaned. "Artemis, darling, you're killing me here."

She smirked at him. "I think you deserve to wait. Just a bit. You did ditch me when I—" Her breath hitched. "When I said I have a son," she soldiered on. Her fingers traced the outside fullness of her breasts before circling underneath, only to skitter up her sternum again.

"Okay. Valid," he said. It was a cruel form of torture, to have her weight heavy on top of his swelling cock, her being half-naked, and yet not being able to touch her. He took a deep breath and let it out slowly. He could be patient.

Spiraling inward, Artemis got closer to the little nubs at the center until she was bumping into the metal sticking out of them. She gasped and her head fell back. *"Finley!"*

"I'm here," he said, his hands twitching on the couch, desperate to reach out to her. "I'm watching. Does it feel good when you play with your piercings?"

"So sensitive," she moaned. "I'm thinking of getting a tattoo," she added.

"Really? What and where?" he asked,

only half his brain able to focus on the question because she was now flicking her fingers over the hard little nubs that were drawing tighter, pebbling as her arousal grew.

"I don't know. Something for Alexander, maybe his name. I'd want it over my heart."

"Fitting. Painful over the ribs, though."

"Do you have any tattoos?" Artemis glanced from his face to his arms; looking for ink, he supposed.

"No. Not as yet. But I can make dragon scales appear whenever and wherever I want." The skin of his left arm rippled and shifted, blue dragon scales appearing in a scattered pattern. He continued it under his shirt sleeve and up the side of his neck, ending behind his ear.

"That is so..." Artemis trailed off, her jaw hanging open.

"Cool?" Finley suggested smugly.

"No. Well, yes. But I was going to say *sexy*," she purred. Artemis stopped playing with her breasts and picked up his arm, touching each scale delicately with her index finger. "Can you feel a difference between these and your skin?"

"The nerve endings are still there," Finley said, a trifle breathlessly. "Just like a tattoo."

"Did you see the cop's tattoo?" she asked, pressing her front against his so that she could reach the scales on his neck. He couldn't decide whether her feather-light touch or the hardness from the barbells was more distracting. "It was like a snake on the back of his hand and up his arm."

Finley froze. "It was *what?*" he demanded urgently, gripping her by her shoulders and pushing her away from him to stare in her eyes. "A snake on his hand?"

"Yes, that's what I said." Artemis's brow furrowed in confusion and she pouted a little from being torn away from him.

"The first kidnapper, the snake shifter, had a snake on his hand. It wasn't the same guy; I would have recognized him. But what are the odds that two guys with similar tattoos wouldn't be after the same thing?" Finley said grimly, half to himself. "I fully bet that the cop was a fake. I'd stake my life on it."

"I'd better call Chloe and let her know the number on the card," Artemis said. She leaned over the edge of the couch to where she'd dropped her purse on the floor. Rather than fish around inside it from that position, she dropped it on the couch where she'd been sitting and dug through it for the business card and her phone. Finding both, she sat comfortably back on his lap, phone set to speaker in between them.

Chloe picked up on the second ring and they told her their suspicions.

"We definitely did not send anyone over to the daycare. Thank you for informing us. We'll be on the lookout for a man matching your description," Chloe said briskly.

They said their goodbyes and Artemis hung up.

"What now?" Finley asked her, using all his will power to keep his eyes above her neck.

"I think we should test Mercury," Artemis said thoughtfully, tapping the edge of her phone against her chin.

Finley's eyebrows rose in surprise. "You mentioned him to the fake cop. But who is he? And why?"

Artemis explained that Mercury had been the reason she was late the evening of the first kidnapping attempt. His excuse had been flimsy and unreasonable. "He left with a threat, but I don't know," Artemis finished. "Kidnapping a child because of a rumor sounds unlikely, even for him."

"It does sound extreme," Finley agreed. "Granted, I don't know the guy."

"Trust me." Artemis tapped out a number and hit the call button.

Mercury picked up on the third ring. "Mercury Delivery Service, you'll think your packages have wings, Mercury speaking. How can I help you?"

"It's Artemis Chase. We need to talk."

Finley heard a squeak and a loud thump before silence.

"Are you still there?" Artemis asked, brow furrowed.

"Yup. Yes. Still here." Mercury was huffing and puffing, scraping noises in the background. "Talk about what, Miss Chase? Did you decide to come clean regarding the expansion of your business into shipping?"

"I prefer the words 'clarifying the situation'. But first, I need a promise from you that you will help me with a problem I have."

"I make no such promises lightly," Mercury scoffed.

Artemis was silent for a minute, biting her lip as she thought. Finley wondered what her thought process was.

"I'm going to take a chance," Artemis muttered. "Mercury, this is off the record to protect my partner. I will not reveal their name. You will have to be satisfied with my account. I am considering the proposal of opening a bank branch on a shipboard casino."

There was silence on the other end. Finally, Mercury said in a strangled voice, "A casino on a *ship*?"

"Yes, that's what I said," Artemis replied impatiently.

"Shipping business, my ass," Mercury growled. "I apologize profusely, Miss Chase. My information was... wildly blown out of proportion. How can I help you?"

"My son has been kidnapped."

Finley was proud of how steadily she stated her problem. He knew she was probably dissociating, but if this helped, then it was necessary.

Mercury was silent again. "I think I was set up to take the fall for this. I assure you, I never involve innocents in *any* of my machinations."

Artemis sighed. "That makes sense. I need your help in finding him."

"Have you received a request for ransom?"

"Not yet."

"If it is a digital transfer, I can trace where the money goes. Don't send it until I can build the tracker code and put it in your account. Even if it's sent to a shell account, I'll be able to get into it. It'll also let me retrieve it for you after you get your son back."

"I don't care about the money!" Artemis shouted. She took a deep breath and Finley put his hand on her knee, offering his silent support. "I need your help to find *him.* You track your packages, don't you? Is it by magic? Can you track him?"

Mercury hmm'd thoughtfully. "Possibly. It would require some tweaking. Let me get back to you."

"Thank you," Artemis breathed before hanging up.

"That went fairly well," Finley said cautiously, watching her closely. She'd dropped her arm holding the phone into her lap, and was staring unseeingly at the wall over his head.

"I might have a bit of hope," Artemis said slowly. "Not much, but a bit."

"Who else knew you were stuck at work when Mercury stalled you?"

"Luna."

Finley raised his eyebrows in question.

Artemis glared at him. "Not a chance," she snapped, sitting straight up.

"Okay. I trust your instincts." He

rubbed his palms along the outside of her thighs soothingly and she softened again. "What now?"

Glancing down at her still half-naked body, Artemis gave a self-deprecating chuckle. "I'm sure you're not in the mood to continue where we left off."

"Why would you think that?"

"Those weren't sexy conversations."

"They were necessary ones." Finley slid his hands behind her knees and pulled her closer. "You're sitting on my lap with your gorgeous breasts on display and won't let me touch you. How do you really think I'm feeling?"

Her eyes widened when she settled over his thick cock and she swallowed hard. "I think you've been very patient," Artemis whispered.

"I have," Finley rumbled.

"Touch me?"

Finley curled his hands around the swell of her ass, leaning forward to pepper light kisses along her collarbones. The taste of her skin immediately overwhelmed him. His hands were everywhere; holding her waist, tracing down her back, cupping her perfect breasts, playing with the sexy little barbells through her nipples with his thumbs...

Artemis arched her back, pressing into his touch with a sigh of pleasure.

"You're so responsive," Finley murmured appreciatively into her skin. He trailed kisses down her chest, licking over one nipple and then the other. "I want to bury my face between your legs and make you scream for me until you can't remember anything but my name."

"Oh god," Artemis moaned.

He drew her nipple into his mouth, biting gently and flicking his tongue over the bud until she rocked against him with a cry.

"Suddenly not so sure sex is off the table," she gasped, writhing over his hard cock.

Fortunately, her phone rang at that moment, so Finley didn't have to wrestle with his conscience over that. He wasn't so sure he'd be able to resist her, not if she was begging him to have sex with her. His will power wouldn't be able to hold out against that torture.

Artemis snatched her phone up from where it had fallen to the couch cushion and accepted the call, putting it on speaker. "Hello?"

"Is this Artemis Chase?" a distorted voice asked.

"Speaking. Is my son all right? Please, tell me he's okay!"

The caller ignored her question. "If you want to see your son again, it'll cost you one million dollars. You have three hours to collect it. I will call back at that time to give you the information to proceed with the digital transfer."

"Can I talk to him, please?" Artemis begged.

There was silence on the other end of the line.

Artemis met Finley's eyes. The depth of her fear was visible within them, cutting him to the core.

"Mom?" whispered a tiny voice.

"Alexander, darling, are you okay?" Artemis asked, clutching her phone tightly.

"Mom, where am I? I want to be at my party."

"I know, baby. When you're back here with me, we can have your party again, okay? Be strong for me. I love you," Artemis said.

"I love you too, Mom!"

Silence again, during which Artemis's body heaved as she struggled to control her tears.

"Will we get our money, or do you need further incentive?" the distorted voice asked.

"You'll get it," Artemis snarled. "Harm one hair on his head and I will not rest until you pay.”

The call disconnected.

“He’s okay!” Artemis gasped, and then burst into tears.

“I’m going to call Chloe,” Finley said. “Can you get a million dollars together in three hours?”

Artemis shook her head and wiped her eyes. “I don’t have that much money, even if I liquidated all my stocks. I guess I need to ask Mercury for another favor.” She shuddered.

“If it’s his money used in the ransom, he’ll be that much more incentivized to get it back,” Finley pointed out with a grin.

“That’s true.” She sniffed. “Where are my glasses? I should probably get dressed. We’re going to have to leave soon anyway."

Reluctantly, Finley removed his hands from her body. "They're over here." He reached out and hooked the arm of her glasses with a finger, holding them up for her.

"Thanks." She got off his lap and grabbed her sweater, her phone already dialing Mercury's number.

Finley let his gaze linger on her while he called Chloe, not wanting their moment to end.

"Go for Chloe."

"Artemis got the ransom call," Finley said, and repeated everything they'd been told slowly so that Chloe could write it down.

Chloe whistled. "Damn, that isn't cheap. What's her plan?"

"She's asking Mercury for a favor." He could practically hear Chloe's eyebrows rise in the silence that followed. "Apparently he has a soft spot for kids."

"I suppose so," Chloe said dubiously. "We'll be ready to go when you get the directions."

"Thank you." He hung up.

"We'll meet you at your office in half an hour," Artemis was saying into her phone.

Finley couldn't hear the other man's response, but that sounded promising. He stretched as he got to his feet and adjusted his cock in his pants. It would deflate soon enough.

Artemis said, "Thank you again," and hung up. "Okay, we should go get my car. His office is on the other side of

Purgatory."

"Or we could fly," Finley said with a shrug. "I'm faster than a car." He frowned.

"What is it?" Artemis asked.

"A speeding car…" He rubbed his chin with a hand. "When I was out walking, a car sped past me. It was going way over the speed limit."

"What did it look like?" Artemis asked.

"Black, nondescript. I wouldn't have remembered it if it hadn't been driving so fast. Do you think it was the kidnapper's car?"

"Don't you?"

"I guess I wouldn't have brought it up if a large part of me didn't think so, huh?" Finley sighed. "No idea how that information would help, though."

"It's possible that it was caught on camera somewhere. I'll call Chloe while we're flying."

Finley chuckled. "I don't think you'll be able to hear her."

CHAPTER THIRTEEN

FINLEY WAS RIGHT, Artemis thought from on top of the lofty height of his dragon. His wings curved gracefully through the air on either side of her.

Although I think it would be difficult to hear her because of all the blood rushing through my ears, rather than the ambient noise of flying.

Instead, she had called Chloe while Finley studied the aerial map of the

Underworld so that he could find Mercury's office.

Chloe had been doubtful that it would pan out, but was grateful for even the slimmest potential lead.

Artemis felt her spirits rise along with the sweep of Finley's wings. It was hard to feel pessimistic when so many people were on her side.

Backwinging, Finley dropped them down in front of a nondescript warehouse. The only thing that differentiated this brick building from the one next to it was the obnoxiously large sign over the main door proclaiming "Mercury Delivery Service" in blocky gray letters on a white background.

Finley squatted as close to the

ground as he could get, and Artemis slid from his back, using his elbow to steady herself. The next instant, he shifted back into his human form. She reached for his hand, needing physical touch to calm down.

"What if he says no?" Her stomach sank into her toes. "What if he's had a change of heart?"

"Then we'll figure it out. We've got time." Finley rubbed his thumb over the back of her hand. "I'm sure Lucifer would be willing to help out."

Artemis made a face. "I'm not sure how I feel about that. At least Mercury has a way of tracking his money and can get it back."

"Then why would he say no?" Finley shrugged and opened the door for her, holding it wide so she could walk through it first.

Artemis had been expecting the warehouse to be dimly lit inside. She wasn't really sure why she'd thought that. Probably because in movies, warehouses were always deserted or rundown. This one was brightly lit, from both lights and skylights spaced out across the roof. The walls were a clean white with the delivery service logo and motto painted brightly across them. People were working in various areas; sorting packages, loading boxes into a truck in the back, filing paperwork, doing something on a computer.

She spotted an office in the nearest corner, the door open, and walked purposefully toward it. Finley kept pace with her, his presence reassuring at her side.

Mercury greeted them distractedly, waving a hand at the chairs across from his desk without looking away from his computer screen. "Still working on the code," he muttered. "Almost got it." He frowned, fingers moving at lightning speed across his keyboard.

From Artemis's position at the door, she could see the lines of code propagating across the screen, faster than she could decipher. Finley nodded at the chairs and she shrugged, silently following orders. Interrupting wouldn't help anyone.

After about five minutes, during which her knee had started bouncing with anxiety until Finley had put his hand overtop, Mercury clicked decisively with the mouse and then focused on them, stretching his fingers one at a time. "I haven't coded like that in years. I'm checking it before I apply it to your account. It's removable after all this." He gestured vaguely in the air. "I don't want to continue to follow your transactions for the rest of our lives!" He laughed loudly at his joke.

Artemis couldn't bring herself to fake a chuckle. "Will this help us find him?"

"Assuredly. The code I've written must be attached to a single dollar. You'll have to empty your account before I attach it, so that we know that the correct dollar gets sent. The code will make your one dollar look like a million dollars in their account. This baby," he patted the top of his monitor confidently, "will dig until it finds every detail needed to bring this guy down. And send all that data to me here." He tossed a phone at her. "I've also already tagged him. Well, his clothing. Can't tag a person. But clothing can be considered a package, right?" He grinned.

Artemis clutched the phone tightly in her hands, looking at the map of Purgatory with the blinking red dot on the far outskirts, the opposite direction from Finley's house. "He's there? Let's go get him!" She stood, her chair scraping backwards with her motion.

Mercury held up a hand. "We need you to do the ransom transfer. We have to get this guy cleanly, or else he might try this again. Do you really want to be looking over your shoulder every second of every day?"

"But..." She could feel the tears welling in her throat. How could she be so close to getting him, and yet not able to go to him?

Finley put his hand on her arm. "We've only got fifteen minutes left until they call with directions. You have to answer."

"You also have to empty your account," Mercury reminded her. "Get going."

Artemis sat again and pulled out her own phone. She put the one with the red dot, Alexander, on the desk where she could keep an eye on it while she logged into her account and moved all her money out of her checking account into her savings account. "Done. What else do you need from me?"

"Your account number," Mercury said, distracted by his screen again. "Code's good. This'll work." He looked up expectantly. It took Artemis a moment to realize that he was waiting for her information. She gave it and he clicked away on his computer for a few minutes. "Done."

"And not a minute too soon," Finley said wryly as her phone rang.

The caller ID was blank. Heart rate kicking up, she answered, "Artemis Chase."

The modified voice, same as the previous one, started speaking in a monotone. "I am going to give you the account number. You will transfer the money. Once we have verified it, we will call you back with the location of your son."

Artemis's gaze flicked to the phone on the desk, the red dot blinking reassuringly at her, as she took the pen Mercury silently handed to her. "All right. I'm ready to write the number down." With a mostly steady hand, she copied the numbers out.

"You have five minutes to get that money into our account," the voice growled, making Artemis shake with fear.

"I already told you I was going to follow your instructions," Artemis snapped, but the line went dead.

Mercury reached for her phone. "I'll transfer it. You two have to go *now*. The code won't hold up if they try to split the money. I'll give you as long as possible."

She grabbed the tracking phone, just in case they decided to move Alexander, before exchanging a glance with Finley. As one, they surged to their feet and took off running for the door.

"I know exactly where that house is," Finley said, unfairly sounding not out of breath. "Time is of the essence."

He scooped her in his arms just outside the door, and she felt the uncomfortable sensation of his shift against her body, her stomach dropping from the sudden change in height and speed. She held onto his claws for dear life as the Underworld streamed past underneath them. Finley was *fast*. It was more than a little terrifying, although she was grateful for it at the moment.

Less than two minutes after she had hung up with the kidnappers, they were landing in the backyard of a run-down house.

Back on her feet, Artemis took two wobbling steps toward the back door, unsure of what to expect from the dilapidated building.

"Let me go first," Finley said in an undertone. "I wish we knew what floor they were keeping him on."

"Actually…"

Finley raised an eyebrow, but Artemis closed her eyes, blocking out distractions. Sending out her power, she felt for the life force of her son. "Main floor. That room." She pointed at a dirty small window to the right of the door.

"There are three others in the house, but none in the room with him." She opened her eyes again, to see Finley looking at her with awe.

"Impressive. And very helpful." Finley paused for a beat. "Okay, here's the plan."

It took him less time to tell her the plan than to break through the back door. She caught sight of the doorknob as she passed it; it was crumpled beyond recognition. Swiftly, they moved through the back hallway into the living room. There were three men sitting on folding chairs. They leapt to their feet when they saw Finley, but Artemis didn't wait around to find out what they did next, turning away from them and running down the hallway to the bedrooms.

A roar, followed by the shattering of glass, met her ears just as she reached the door she wanted. It was locked.

Of course it is.

Artemis knocked on the door and put her mouth to the edge where the door met the frame. "Alexander? It's Mom. I'm going to get you out of here. Hang on, sweetheart."

"Mom?" Alexander called back. "I'm scared, Mom!"

"Be brave, dear one. I'm coming." She bent over to examine the knob. It was a standard key lock mechanism. With no key hanging next to the door, Artemis had no choice. She put her hand over the knob and pressed her power inside, forming the shape of a key and forcing the lock open.

It clicked loudly, even over the noise of the fight down the hall, and she pushed open the door. Artemis ran inside and fell to her knees in front of Alexander, scooping him up in her arms and cradling him like the baby he used to be. "I'm so sorry, I love you," she found herself babbling into his curls as he shook with sobs in her arms. "Are you okay?"

"I did the finger thing Lee taught me," Alexander said, hiccupping softly. "It helped."

"Good for you. Let's get you out of here." She didn't want to let him go ever again, but she asked, "Would you rather walk or be carried?"

Alexander tightened his grip around her neck with his little arms. "Don't put me down, please, Mom," he said brokenly.

"I've got you," she replied automatically. Getting to her feet was a bit of a struggle. She must have used more power than she realized to open the lock. Her energy was vastly depleted.

Once standing, she cautiously peeped out into the hallway. The fight was still going on in the living room, based on the loud crashes and yells she could hear. At least she hadn't heard any gunshots.

Artemis walked as quickly as she could to the back hallway, but when she reached the corner, she stopped, frozen by the sight of the fight in the living room.

Well, more like in the front yard.

The entire front wall and window of

the living room were gone, as if a very large creature had been thrown through it. Finley had shifted into his dragon form, and was fighting two snake shifters and...

"*Jormund?*" Artemis gasped, hardly able to believe her eyes. In his snake god form, Jormund Blanca was ginormous, even bigger than Finley's dragon form. Jormund was strong and fast, but even though Finley had experience in the fighting ring, he was used to fighting one opponent at a time. *This* fight didn't look good.

There was no time to call for backup. Artemis was the only one who could save him. She looked down at the little boy in her arms and bit her lip.

Would he get hurt if she interfered?

In her moment of indecision, the choice was made for her.

Twin roars echoed through the neighborhood as Finley's brothers arrived, launching themselves at the smaller snake shifters and leaving Finley to deal with the snake god.

Hera, with beautiful white wings, landed at the opening of the house. "Come," she said, holding her hand out to Artemis. "There is nothing you can do here."

"Like shit there isn't!" Artemis said. "Take Alexander to Maddie. I don't want him harmed. And call Chloe, please."

"She's already on her way," Hera said. "Alexander, will you come with me?"

"Please, go with Hera," Artemis encouraged him. "I need to save Lee."

"Okay, Mom." Alexander reached out for Hera and transferred to the other Goddess easily.

"I love you," Artemis said.

"Love you!" His last word was cut off as Hera sprang upward, her big beautiful wings catching a draft and speeding them skyward.

Artemis sucked in a deep breath and squared her shoulders. She could see the moon rising early, the sun still high in the sky. It wouldn't be as powerful a statement as it would have been at night, but she would make do.

Weaving the moonbeam into a rope, she looped the length of it in one hand, the other holding the noose she had made with it. She centered herself in the opening and shouted, "Jormund! You have betrayed me for the last time. Stop this at once!" She threw the noose at Jormund's head, guided by the moonbeams, and it settled around his jaw, snapping his mouth shut.

She wrenched his head around, pulling on the rope she still held, until he was facing her directly. The flash of recognition in his eyes was almost amusing to see. "Call off your men," Artemis growled.

Jormund shifted slowly back into his human form, the noose shrinking with him and settling around his neck, not too tight. "Xavier, Maksim, stop," he said weakly. "It's over."

"Damn right it's over," Artemis snapped. "What on Earth, on Purgatory, were you thinking? Kidnapping? For ransom?" She seethed for a moment. "Your own son, whom you haven't seen… *ever?*"

"Come on, baby—" Jormund started.

Artemis cut him off, eyes blazing with light as well as anger. "You don't have the right to call me that. You lost it a long time ago, when you ran away," she hissed, tightening the noose. "How *dare* you kidnap my son!"

"I had to, if I wanted to see him," Jormund whined.

"Bullshit!" Artemis growled. "You had an invite to his birthday party, just as you have every year. You could have arranged to see him any time you wanted. But this isn't about him. This is about *money.*" She spat the word in his face and he flinched. "Or did you forget that you asked for a ransom?"

"I *had* to," Jormund begged. "I owe a lot of people a lot of money."

"Now, *that* is not my problem." The sound of sirens in the distance filled the air. "And it won't be yours for much longer either."

Jormund's face turned pale.

"I hope I never lay eyes on you again." Artemis turned away from him as he fell to his knees amidst the rubble. Finley had shifted back into his human form, not looking much worse for having been in an all-out brawl with the snake god. She sighed, relieved.

When Chloe arrived, Artemis unraveled her rope once Jormund was taken into custody.

And even though he begged her to

help him, she didn't acknowledge his existence or even look away from Finley.

Jormund didn't deserve a single second of her attention. Not anymore.

She threw herself at Finley, hugging him for all she was worth. "I was so worried for you," she whispered. "I didn't think you'd win that fight."

Finley made a disgruntled noise in his throat. "I probably wouldn't have without help," he admitted.

Jaden and Augustine flew them both back to Maddie's. Finley was too sore to fly back. He said his wings had been torn. Artemis wasn't sure if that manifested anywhere on his human form, but it sounded painful no matter what.

Alexander greeted them with a

running hug, launching himself into her arms.

"You were so brave," Artemis murmured to him. "I'm so proud of you!"

"Mom?"

"Yes, my darling?"

"Can we go home?"

"Of course." Artemis stood and held her hand out to him.

"Can Lee come too?"

Artemis and Finley exchanged shy glances.

"I would like that," Artemis said quietly.

"Then I will join you," Finley agreed readily.

They spent the rest of the day playing games in Artemis's backyard before making dinner.

"It is time for bed, young man," Artemis said after Alexander almost fell asleep in his bowl of spaghetti. "You've had a busy day."

"But I'm not—" Alexander yawned widely, "—tired!"

Finley chuckled. "Maybe you're not, but your mother used a lot of power today, and I'm beat. So it's probably best that you go to bed so we can rest."

Artemis smiled ruefully. "That's true."

Alexander finally agreed and Artemis followed him upstairs to his room. "Stay? Please?" she whispered to Finley before she left the living room.

He nodded.

"Mom?" Alexander asked, climbing into bed.

"Yes, sweetheart?" Artemis curled up

around his small body, holding him close.

"Will I get taken away again?"

Artemis's heart broke. "No. No, baby, you won't. Those men are going to jail for a very long time. You're safe." She stroked his silky curls with one hand.

"Thank you for finding me."

"I would have searched to the ends of the Earth for you," Artemis promised him, kissing his forehead. "I love you."

"Can we have my birthday tomorrow instead?" Alexander asked.

"Of course."

"With pancakes again?"

Artemis chuckled. "Yes, with pancakes."

"Maybe Lee would like pancakes too? Can you ask him for me?"

"You want him to eat breakfast with us tomorrow morning?" Artemis asked.

Alexander yawned and cuddled his bear tighter. "Every morning."

"Goodnight, sweetheart. I'll ask him." She kissed his cheek gently. He was already asleep.

Artemis got out of his bed, careful not to wake him, and crossed the hall into her room to retrieve the monitor before heading back downstairs. Even though Finley had said he would stay, she was still relieved to hear the clink of dishes in the kitchen.

"I promise my life isn't usually this dramatic," she said from the doorway and then stopped short at the sight before her eyes. "Finley!" she gasped.

CHAPTER FOURTEEN

FINLEY WONDERED WHAT was going through Artemis's mind when she pleaded with him to stay, those shining silver eyes of hers fixating on him before she followed Alexander upstairs to his room.

Sure, she wanted him to stay.

Was she feeling nervous about being alone?

Did she need a friend to talk to?

Was she going to continue where they left off at his house that morning?

Goosebumps prickled over his skin at that thought. She'd been so hot, sitting half-naked on top of him.

He gave himself a shake.

Don't get ahead of yourself.

To distract himself, he ran the water into the sink and squirted dish soap in, making a small mound of bubbles. He worked his way through plates and cups before moving on to the pots and pans. The quiet ritual of cleaning up the kitchen was a balm to the turmoil in his brain.

As much as he wanted Artemis, he wanted to be there for her even more. Whatever she needed from him, he would give her. Even if it meant giving her space.

He finished washing the last dish and found the drying cloth, hunting through her cupboards for the correct location to place the dishes.

The stairs creaked slightly when he was almost done, warning him of her arrival. He turned at her greeting and smirked at her slack-jawed expression.

"You didn't have to do all this," Artemis said weakly, waving a hand around the kitchen.

"I know. I wanted to help, and this was the only thing I could think of. Where do you keep your frying pan?" He nodded at it; he'd put it on the kitchen table.

"Might as well leave it out," Artemis said with a shake of her head. "I'm going to need it to make pancakes for Alexander tomorrow. He wants a do-over of his birthday. I can't say that I blame him."

To Finley's horror, her chin wobbled and her face scrunched up, tears running down her cheeks.

"Who would want their third birthday to be marred by being kidnapped?" she gasped, wrapping her arms around her middle as if she was holding herself together.

Finley put down the dish and cloth and was across the kitchen in two long strides, scooping her up in his arms and tucking her head under his chin. "He was also rescued," he murmured, rocking her slightly.

"He shouldn't have needed to be!" she

cried. "I can't *believe* that asshole! Kidnapping a child for ransom? His *own* child?"

"He didn't know him. Alexander is not his child. He's yours. And you protected him."

"I let him get taken. How did they manage it?" She started to shake in his arms. It felt like she was going into shock.

He adjusted his hold on her, looser around the ribs, protective cage along her back with his forearms. "Invisibility spell, most likely." Finley sighed heavily. "Expensive, but effective."

"I'll talk to Maddie about putting spell-blockers around the daycare," Artemis muttered, wiping under her glasses. "We don't want that sort of thing happening again."

"Good idea." Finley curled one hand around her neck. "Can you focus for me for a second? Tell me about one thing you see. Something special."

"The clock on the wall."

Finley looked up at the hideous rooster clock.

"I hate it." A giggle escaped her. "But it was gifted to me by my brother, Apollo. I don't see him very often, but every time he visits, he looks up at it. If I got rid of it, he'd notice immediately."

"Maybe he gave it to you because it's so awful and he wants to see how long it'll take for you to get rid of it," Finley said with a chuckle. "Do you want to smash it?"

"Yes! No! I don't know." Artemis bit

her lip indecisively.

"Sleep on it. Buy a new one and then you can smash it," Finley suggested. "It was just an idea. I always feel better after I go through my exercise routine, and I wasn't sure if you had another physical outlet."

Artemis pulled back a little and smirked up at him. "I can think of a much more satisfying way to exert myself."

Finley blew out a long breath. "I wasn't sure you'd want—"

"Want you?" Artemis interrupted him incredulously. "Are you kidding me right now? You—" She sucked in a deep breath. "Follow me."

She led him into her living room and pushed him down on her couch, straddling his thighs a second later. She took his face in her hands.

"You've been looking after my son for two weeks now. Every day that you've been at the daycare, Alexander has come home practically bubbling over with stories about Lee, about *you*. I've been falling in love with you through Alexander's stories. And today? You've been as strung out as I have. You combed the city for him. You fought three guys so I could rescue him. You've been with me every step of the way. I couldn't want you more than I do in this very instant."

"Falling in love?" Finley said breathlessly. His brain felt fuzzy, hearing her say that. He needed to hear it again. "You're in love with me?"

Artemis blushed. "Yes, I rather think I am."

"Can I kiss you?"

"If you don't, I might have to do something drastic."

God—no, *Goddess*, he loved this woman.

"Hmm, I don't know. I kinda like it when you do something drastic," he teased.

Artemis smirked at him. "Then you'll love this." Her hands left the sides of his face to curl around the back of his head, bringing his mouth to hers.

The kiss started out tentative, her soft lips brushing gently against his, but they grew more insistent as time went on. Her tongue slipped into his mouth, dancing with his.

He felt dizzy, all the blood in his body rushing down between his legs, her weight and warmth directly on top of him. "Artemis," he murmured, cupping her ass in his hands and encouraging her to rock her hips.

"Ohhh," Artemis groaned, grinding down against the fly of his jeans while she gasped against his skin. "I want to see you." Her hands slipped under his shirt, yanking it up his torso.

He helped her take it the rest of the way off, reluctantly removing his hands from her body. The instant he took over with his shirt, she went for his belt and zipper, opening them with nimble fingers, tugging them aside and growling when she couldn't get an opening large enough.

Finley chuckled. "Hang on. Let me stand up for a sec."

Shifting onto the floor on her knees between his spread thighs, she blinked up at him innocently.

He groaned and put one hand through her hair. "Fuck," he whispered. "Seeing you like this... I'm not going to last long."

"That's okay. I'm out of practice and my jaw will probably get tired," she teased.

Trying not to think about that, Finley stood and pushed his jeans and underwear over his ass. She enthusiastically pulled them the rest of the way down to his ankles before grabbing his cock and licking up the underside with gusto. At the head, she swirled her tongue around the crown and swallowed his length until he felt the back of her throat. His knees shook.

"Gotta sit," he croaked.

She hummed acknowledgement and followed him back down to the couch, starting up a rhythm bobbing her head over him, her saliva dripping out the corners of her mouth.

He *really* wasn't going to last long. "*Artemis*," he gasped. Finley traced her jaw with the fingers of one hand, feeling the stretch at the joint. "Going to come," he warned her.

She hummed again and deepened her strokes, taking him all the way to the root. He could see her throat expanding around his cock and it set him off, his balls tucking up against his body, tingles exploding along his nerve endings from his scalp to his toes. His fists clenched tight, his head thrown back on the couch, he shot down her throat, overwhelmed by the surge of pleasure.

Artemis wiped delicately at the corner of her mouth when she moved from the floor back onto his lap. "Was that okay?"

"Okay?" Finley squeaked, feeling liquefied. "That doesn't even come close to describing it."

Smirking, Artemis got to her feet. "There's a lot more where that came from, if you want."

Recovering swiftly, Finley yanked her by her hand onto his lap, crushing her against him. "Oh, I *want*," he growled. "I want you to be my mate. I want forever."

She shivered in his hold, her jaw

dropping a little.

He searched her gaze.

Had he gone too far too fast?

But her silver eyes were shining with hope, not fear, so he tilted her head slightly with one large hand—he felt so big when he was around her—and tipped his chin to press their lips together. She surrendered to him immediately, welcoming him into her mouth. Finley tasted his essence on her tongue and his head spun at the very thought of how it got there.

He pulled back from her slightly, their breathing ragged as it washed over their skin. "Take off your clothes," he rasped, barely recognizing his voice.

Her pupils dilated further, almost swallowing the silver. In a heartbeat, her sweater was off, knocking her glasses askew, and halfway across the room as she flung it away.

Enthusiastically, Finley cupped her breasts, using fingers, tongue, lips, and teeth to draw little sighs, moans, and cries of pleasure from her. "You are so fucking hot," he breathed against her sternum. "These..." He pulled lightly on the barbells. "Are my absolute favorite thing ever."

"I can tell," Artemis moaned. "Feels so good, you have no idea." She rocked her hips and Finley was surprised to note that his erection had returned full force. "Finley, I need you inside me now. We can talk about the mate thing later."

"Pants," he said urgently, slipping them over her ass as far as he could with her straddling him.

She stood up to obey him, but the doorbell rang before he could strip her. She groaned. "Not now!"

"Could be important," Finley pointed out. He handed her his shirt and pulled his pants off one foot and then the other. "And it could wake Alexander."

Artemis yanked on his shirt, which fell to mid-thigh and slipped off one shoulder, with a glare. "I'm *going*!" She stalked over to the front door beside the living room, unlocked it with a quick flick of her wrist, and threw it open. "Mercury!" she gasped. "Did you get everything you needed?"

Mercury's voice drifted in through the open door, "Yep. This guy is going away for a long time. I wanted to return your phone. Someone named Luna has been calling all day."

"Oh my god, I completely forgot to let her know we got Alexander back!" Artemis cried, taking her phone. "Thank you so much! Let me get you yours."

Finley dug through the pockets of his jeans and found the phone Mercury had given them with the tracker. He brought it to the door himself, looming beside Artemis like a naked shadow. "Thanks for your help finding her son today," he said.

Mercury grinned. "No problem, and you have nothing to worry about here. I was going to go as soon as Artemis checked that all her accounts were in order." Looking back at her, he added, "I promise I didn't touch a cent of your money, other than the dollar you gave your permission for me to attach the clone code to. The code has been removed completely, and there is no tracking information or anything else of the sort in your phone. It was as if I was never there. God's honor."

Artemis squinted at him. "I know exactly how that kind of honor works."

"So you know that if I'm lying, I will suffer," Mercury said solemnly. "I swear it."

She nodded. "Thank you."

Mercury turned to leave, but gave Finley one last long look from head to toe. "Oh, and Artemis, don't impale yourself too hard. Sitting hurts like a bitch after something like that."

Finley snorted. "Good night." He

closed the door and found Artemis flicking through her text messages on her phone.

"Luna is going to kill me if I don't call her. I'm a terrible boss and an even worse friend," Artemis complained.

"So call her. I'm a little hungry. Can I make you something while you're on the phone?"

"Grilled cheese?"

Finley chuckled. "Sure thing. I'm just going to cover up while doing anything near a stovetop."

Artemis pouted. "Do you have to?"

"I do if I don't want burns on a very sensitive area."

"Ugh, fine!" Artemis replied playfully. "Put on your underwear or something. Hide that beautiful cock away."

Finley pulled her into his arms. "I'll hide it away again and again inside your body until you're incoherent but for my name," he whispered fervently. "Until then, you must wait."

She opened and closed her mouth a couple times before a tiny squeak escaped. "Okay."

"Now, go call Luna." He slapped her ass playfully. "Reassure her that all is well and you were distracted by your naked boyfriend."

Her face lit up. "Boyfriend?"

"Call Luna," he ordered again, as sternly as he was capable when faced with her beauty. He scooped up his underwear and headed for the kitchen and started making the grilled cheese sandwiches. Snippets of Artemis's conversation with Luna filtered in from the other room; apologies, details of the rescue, his name more than once, as well as sobs and chuckles. It had been a tough day for Artemis. Her emotions were all over the place. Finley made up his mind not to bring up mating again tonight.

It turned out he didn't have to.

Artemis entered the kitchen without her phone and wrapped her arms around his waist from behind. "You said you wanted to be mates. What does that entail, exactly?"

"It's a promise. More than marriage, for my people. We pledge ourselves to each other, and I give you a mating bite at the peak of ecstasy." Finley closed his eyes. "It's okay. You don't have to decide tonight. It's an important decision, and I don't want you to make it lightly."

Humming into his bare shoulder blade, Artemis squeezed her arms tighter around his waist. "But you can have sex without being mated, right?"

Finley's lips quirked up into a smirk, even though she couldn't see his face. "Is that a roundabout way of asking if I'm a virgin?"

Artemis chuckled. "I hadn't thought of it like that. No, I was just making sure we could still have sex tonight, even if I don't decide right away."

"Don't worry. We can still have sex." Finley attempted to block out the mental image of Artemis riding his cock, with mixed results. At this rate, he was going to be half-hard all evening.

"That's good." He felt her head shift, and then she let out a little cry of dismay. "Is that my *face*?" She left him to walk over to the window, reflective now that the sun had set.

Finley glanced at her, taking in the mascara running down her cheeks. "You've had a stressful day."

"Yes, but look at me!" Artemis wailed. "How could you possibly want me when I look like this?"

Frowning, Finley moved the pan off the burner, not wanting to char the grilled cheese, and cupped her face in his hands. He gently brushed her hair back. "You've never looked more beautiful."

She scoffed and tried to pull away, but he didn't let her.

"Your tears are ones of shock and relief. Only a mother as amazing as you could shed these. And that makes you the most beautiful woman I've ever seen, even with your makeup not in the right place."

Artemis stared up at him, her mouth gaping. "Yes."

Finley's brain stalled. "Sorry, yes? Yes to what?"

"Yes, I want to be your mate." She said it calmly, almost matter-of-factly, the complete opposite to what those words felt like in his brain.

"Holy shit," he murmured, making her giggle. He kissed her upturned lips. "Holy shit!" he said again, slightly less dazedly. "Really?"

"Yes, really. I love you. You love me.

You love my son. We'll work through anything else that comes up together." She beamed up at him.

"Sounds perfect to me." He kissed her again, deepening the kiss until she moaned and swayed against him. "One thing left to do," he whispered.

"Have sex?"

"Eat these grilled cheese sandwiches I've been slaving over."

"Oh, for just minutes!" she said sarcastically.

"Hey, I'll have you know that I painstakingly cut each piece of cheese to the same exact size!" he protested.

She raised an eyebrow. "You don't cook much, do you?"

"No." Finley blushed. "Does it show?"

"Just a bit." Artemis patted his arm.

"It's okay. I'll help teach you. So will Alexander."

"I look forward to it."

He finished making their snack and they ate it at the kitchen table, trading glances that made his skin burn for her touch.

After Artemis had chewed her last bite, she got to her feet and said, "I'm going to go wash my face."

"I'll clean up here," Finley said.

"It can wait until tomorrow," she said impatiently.

"Hey…" He took her hand. "We've got time. You go wash, and I'll wash here. Do you want me to meet you in your room, or are you coming back out?"

Artemis seemed speechless for a moment. "Come to my room, please."

"Gladly."

He had never washed dishes so quickly, thoughts of Artemis waiting for him filling his head. He turned off the lights behind him, checked the front door was locked, and headed for the door with the light glowing underneath.

He pushed it open and his jaw dropped.

CHAPTER FIFTEEN

ARTEMIS FELT LIKE a schoolgirl with a crush as she headed into her bathroom. Her stomach was filled with butterflies, and she couldn't wipe the giddy grin from her face.

Until she caught a glimpse of herself in the mirror and almost shrieked with surprise. The windows in the kitchen had not done the melting of her mascara justice. A wild giggle escaped her lips.

"At least Finley has seen me at my worst," she told her reflection. "And he loves me." She wrapped her arms around her body as if she could hold the emotion tight to her heart. "We're going to be mates!"

She waited for the sinking feeling to seep in, for panic to overwhelm her. Neither happened, and she did a little dance right there in her bathroom before taking a few deep breaths to calm down.

The dried makeup was a pain to clean off, and she had to use a special solution that Hera had mixed up for her to get the last of it off her skin. Artemis splashed her face a few times, sighing with relief at the feeling of clean water on bare skin, before stripping out of her clothes. She dropped her leggings and underwear into the hamper in the bathroom, but left Finley's shirt on the countertop.

Soap and more water under her arms, wiping away the stress of the day, and then another splash at her more sensitive areas, just to clean things up, since Finley seemed to like eating her out.

Who was she kidding?

She liked it too.

After tidying up the bathroom, she scurried down the hall to her bedroom, Finley's shirt in her arms, hoping that he wasn't close to being finished cleaning up downstairs. After closing the door behind her, she found a box of condoms that hadn't yet expired in her side table and put them on top for easy access, along with a bottle of lube. She put his shirt on the end of the bed and then turned her attention to her own attire.

"Oh my gosh, I have nothing to wear!" she gasped. She felt a little silly; obviously Finley would strip her as soon as possible if she was wearing something, but she wanted to look nice for him. Give him something to unwrap beforehand.

Artemis pulled open her underwear drawer, scowling at the simple panties before digging out her one black thong. She pulled it on, hopping on one leg and then the other.

There wasn't really anything that she could put on the top half of herself, though. Sighing, she picked out a white camisole and slipped into it. She heard

Finley's heavy tread on the stairs and flung herself onto her bed, arranging her body in what she hoped was a seductive position and glancing at the baby monitor.

Alexander was sound asleep, his face turned toward the camera and his bum up in the air.

The door opened and her attention turned to the man framed in the doorway. He was staring at her like she'd hung the moon.

Which, well... That was fitting.

She ran her fingers up her thigh to her hipbone, playing with the thin strip of material there. "Are you going to come in, or..." She let the question hang in the air between them, his gaze fixed on her moving hand.

Finley gave his head a shake as if dispelling cobwebs and took a couple steps into the room, closing the door behind him. "You are stunning," he whispered, crawling up her bed between her legs. He dropped kisses along her outer thigh until he reached where she was playing, alternating between kissing the delicate bone of her hip and sucking lightly on her fingers.

Artemis shivered pleasantly, goosebumps erupting, originating from his lips. "Are you going to take off your underwear?" she asked him to distract herself.

His mouth curved in a smile against her skin. "Maybe," he teased. "I think I want you a little more desperate first."

She pouted and dragged her foot

along his side, hooking her toes in the elastic band at his waist and attempting to tug down.

"Minx," Finley growled. He gripped the sides of her thong. "Can I rip these off you?"

Artemis hesitated. "They're my only black pair."

"I'll replace them."

"Okay." She was surprised by her boldness, and then again by how wet she got from the sound of ripping filling the air. "Oh my God!"

"Not a God, just a dragon shifter," Finley replied cheekily.

He flipped them over somehow and she belatedly remembered that his real job wasn't in a daycare, but in a fighting ring. She looked down at him between her legs, and flushed like a teenager when she realized what he was going to do.

He tossed her destroyed thong somewhere and curled his hands possessively around her upper thighs, pulling her down against his mouth.

Her arms shook as she tried to hold herself up, groaning through the onslaught of pleasure that Finley was providing. When her elbows bent, she took the last reserves of her energy and pushed herself up into a sitting position.

It gave Finley even better access, and he hummed appreciatively as he vigorously lashed his tongue across her swollen clit, setting her off on her first orgasm of the night.

Artemis came down from the height of

ecstasy slowly due to the continuous rolling of his tongue against the most sensitive areas inside her.

Her second orgasm came out of nowhere, and she clapped her hands over her mouth to stifle her cry of surprise, rocking her hips over his face as she rode his tongue. *"Finley!"* she moaned, voice muffled.

This time when she was recovering, Finley manipulated her body down until she was sitting over his hips, his cock thick against her wet folds, only one thin layer of material between them.

She fell forward, hovering over him face to face. She could see her juices all over his lips and chin. The scent was intoxicating. "You feel so good, even with a layer between us," she purred, rolling her pelvis along his length. "Can you feel me hot against you? Can you feel me soaking the fabric?"

Finley's jaw clenched and he nodded once, abruptly. His fingers dimpled the skin of her hips as he forced her down against him repeatedly.

Artemis locked eyes with him, taking in the dilated pupils nearly swallowing the dark blue of his iris. "I want you," she whispered.

"I *need* you," he replied, his voice so full of desire that she shivered. "But first, I want to see you."

Without hesitation, she sat up, ready to whip off her camisole, but he stopped her with his hands on her arms.

"Let me," he said, and she fell back onto all fours hovering over him. "This is one of my favorite parts," he murmured, gently tracing the straps of her top down over the softness of her breasts. He got to the nipples and tugged on the filmy material, her breasts spilling out over the neckline of the top, pressed together and swinging slightly from gravity. "Look how turned on you are, all drawn in tight for me. So sexy." He arched up, sucking one and then the other into his mouth.

As much as she loved the foreplay, Artemis had had enough. She wanted him inside her, like, yesterday. Fortunately, there was a moonbeam falling into her room through the uncovered window. With barely a thought, she twisted it into position between them and shoved the elastic of his underwear down, releasing his cock to the air.

"What?" Finley mumbled, startled.

"I'll take you bare if you don't get this show on the road," Artemis promised fervently. "Is that sufficient begging?"

His lips quirked up in a smirk. "That'll do."

Finley released her and she sat up, whipping her shirt over her head, now completely bare on top of him. The feel of his hard cock twitching against her sensitive flesh made her eyes roll back in her head. "You feel so good," she gasped.

"I'll feel even better inside you," he growled in reply.

Artemis shuddered in agreement. With great strength of will, she pulled herself away from him, getting off the bed to retrieve the condom box. "Take those off," she ordered.

Finley pushed his underwear down and off, and moved up the bed to center himself, all without looking away from her. "You're so hot."

"Even struggling to open a box?" Artemis said with a chuckle, the box torn across the top in her haste to get inside.

"As long as you don't destroy the condom when you open it, seeing you so desperate only turns me on more." He stroked his cock with one large hand and let out a hiss of pleasure. "Now get that thing on me and ride me until we both come so hard I can't see straight."

Amusement blossomed in her chest as she carefully opened the foil packet.

"Will it fit?"

"They're stretchy. Lube me up first. Uh..." He put a hand on her shoulder, stopping her from sucking him into her mouth. "As much as I love your mouth on me, I meant it literally. Saliva dries up, lube is forever."

That prompted a giggle to escape her lips. "I think the phrase is 'diamonds are forever'." She slicked his cock, her fingers barely fitting around it, and felt herself get wetter in anticipation.

"Ehhh," Finley said, arching his back and clenching his fists. "They can be crushed with enough pressure."

"Like the sun," Artemis retorted, rolling the condom down his length with slight difficulty.

"And I plan to make you burn hotter

than the sun for me, baby," he quipped, reaching for the lube. "Get up here."

"That's a half-decent line." Artemis straddled him once more. She moaned as Finley's slicked up fingers rubbed over her folds, sliding inside one at a time.

"There is nothing decent about what I want to do with you," he growled.

She whimpered, rocking her hips to coax him to thrust his fingers harder. "Then do it."

"Don't want to hurt you," he replied through clenched teeth. "Feels so tight."

"I'll stretch. Come on, let me take control," Artemis begged, taking his fingers right to the root. "I may be out of practice with the real thing, but remind me to show you my toy collection sometime."

"That sounds like fun," Finley replied, pulling his hands away from her. "Do you need help positioning— Nevermind," he groaned the last word as she lined him up and sank onto the head.

"Ohhhh, fuck," Artemis gasped, dropping both hands to his chest to brace herself. "You feel so damn good." After the initial breach, her body relaxed and he slid a couple inches inside her. She curled her fingernails into his pectorals and arched her back, taking him in even further.

"Will you be able to move?" Finley asked, his voice sounding strangled. "You feel amazing, but I'm not used to just lying here."

"It's your turn to be patient," Artemis

teased. "Just... give me a second..." She sat up as straight as she was able, taking the rest of him until she felt his coarse pubic hair tickle her clit. Her head fell back, mouth open in a silent moan, unable to make a sound over the sparkles in her nervous system. Her channel rippled around him, squeezing her pleasure at being filled so completely.

Finley's hands flew to her hips. "What you do to me, woman," he rasped. "Just when I think you can't get sexier, you blow me away again."

Artemis cracked a lazy smile at that. "I'm just trying to adjust to having my insides rearranged by your dragon cock."

"That's not my dragon cock. It's very different." Finley smirked up at her and her jaw dropped at the insinuation.

She shook the erotic mental images away, focusing on the present.

The very *full* present.

Finley put his hand over her lower belly and twitched inside her, making her whimper. "I can see the bulge of me inside you," he whispered reverently.

"You like that?" Artemis strained upward, thigh muscles working, only to slam down, taking him to the hilt.

Eyes flaring ice blue for a moment, Finley took control, surging up to join her in a seated position. "You overestimate my strength of will," he growled. Banding his arms around her waist, he flipped them in a smooth motion.

And then he started pounding into

her.

The slapping of their flesh together echoed in her room, the slick providing the perfect counterpoint on each outward motion.

Artemis felt wild, desired, shattered into tiny pieces and put back together again to be made whole... Her world had narrowed to a focus, and it was all on this man and how he made her feel.

She came again, hard, eyes slamming shut and back arching from too much pleasure, too much emotion. When she recovered, she realized that Finley had slowed his strokes and was blinking rapidly.

"Are you okay?" she asked, concerned. "Did something get in your eye?"

"You flared brighter than usual that time," he answered, lowering his head to lick at her collarbone. "I wasn't expecting it. How are you feeling?"

"Amazing," she said happily.

"Are you ready for the big finale?" He swallowed hard, his gaze piercing in its intensity. "Are you sure you want to be mated to me?"

"I'm one hundred percent sure," she reassured him. "What do I need to do?"

"Let me bite you." Finley bared his teeth, and she noticed that they looked slightly sharper than usual. "You just relax and let the orgasm take you."

Artemis chuckled. "I can do that. Oooh—" she broke off.

"What?"

"That last thrust hit pretty— Oh God,

yes!— spectacularly. Yes, right there!" A small corner of her mind remembered that she had to keep her cries quiet so as not to wake Alexander, but it was getting harder and harder to care. "Next time, Luna is babysitting at her house," Artemis said with a moan.

"Oh?" Finley looked smug.

She wished she could wipe that expression off his face, but her nerves were starting to spark again, her muscles tightening in anticipation of release. "Let's just say that I don't get the urge to scream out my dildo's name."

"And that would be?"

"Don't make me say it."

Finley stopped moving, cock almost completely outside of her, just stretching her opening. "Artemis, what is your dildo's name?"

She writhed on the bed, the loss of sensation sending her nerve endings misfiring. "Mani," she said at last, when Finley remained unmoving.

His eyebrows rose. "Old Norse for 'moon'?"

"*Of course* you know Old Norse," she said, exasperated. "Yes, okay?"

"So sometimes, you come in here..." He started a slow, undulating rhythm meant purely to torment her, she was sure of it. "And take out your dildo so you can *fuck the moon*? Or do you bring it outside and fuck yourself in your backyard, clad only in the light of the moon?"

"This is why I didn't want to tell you," she groaned, covering her face with her hands.

"Oh no, this only makes you more interesting. *The* Artemis Chase, CEO of the Underworld's only bank, and she gets off on the moon," Finley teased.

"It's more intense than by myself," Artemis muttered. "Just fuck me already."

"We're not fucking, sweetheart, can't you tell the difference?"

Artemis gaped at him. "What?"

Finley leaned in close to her ear. "I'm making love to you," he whispered, sending goosebumps rippling across her skin.

In fact, his whisper also set off her climax, and she threw her head back as far as she was able, her legs tightening their grip on his thighs.

"You're so beautiful. I love you, Artemis," Finley gasped, and then he bit her hard where her shoulder met her neck as he gushed into the thin barrier of latex between them.

She cried out, the pain-pleasure overwhelming her caution. Her fingernails dug into Finley's shoulder blades, desperate to cling to him. Her vision flared white behind her closed eyelids and she knew she was glowing again.

Artemis gasped a deep breath, confused for a moment as to why her lungs were screaming. Then she realized that she'd been wound so tight that she'd unconsciously been holding her breath. She melted into the mattress and wove her fingers into Finley's hair, holding his head to her neck. He had stopped biting her, and was softly licking over the wounds, sending tingles southward. Her inner walls rippled, an aftershock of the intense orgasm, and Finley groaned into her skin.

"You are so fantastic," he breathed, pulling back to look at her. "You're glowing again."

"Sorry." She felt flustered. She hadn't even known that she *could* glow in the afterglow—*Well, at least that makes sense,* she thought wildly—before Finley.

"Don't you dare apologize. My greatest wish is for you to be so happy that you glow all the time, even when I'm not with you." He peppered kisses along her jaw until he reached her mouth, drawing her into a passionate kiss that had her head spinning. "I love you, all of you." His lips moved down her sternum, over the soft fullness of her breasts, lazily alternating between one side and the other, tonguing at the barbells that pierced her skin.

Finally, Artemis cried out from overstimulation and came again, shaking underneath him, clenching down on his thickness that was still inside her and growing harder by the second. "You need to deal with the first condom," she managed to tell him.

He smirked down at her, the tendons in his forearms standing out against his smooth skin. "Are you sure you're ready for that?"

"Don't be condescending and get another damn condom," Artemis snapped, sticking her tongue out at him.

"As you wish, my mate," Finley said, kissing her lips once more before rolling off the bed.

Artemis felt the ache of no longer having him within her keenly and whimpered at the loss. "Please hurry," she begged, her fingers arrowing down her body to play with her clit and hungry opening. "I need you inside me."

"Not making this easy on me, love," Finley said with a chuckle, his fingers fumbling with the condom packet.

"Well, I want you to be *hard*," she teased, eyeing his cock and licking her lips.

Finley chuckled and gestured down his body. "Already there. I would've thought you'd want me *easy* too." He finally managed to open the condom wrapper and roll it on.

"Only easy for me," she purred, opening her arms to him as he crawled back on top of her.

"That's a guarantee," he whispered, sliding home again and making both of them groan.

"Love you!" Artemis gasped.

"Forever," Finley promised as he moved within her.

EPILOGUE

A couple months later...

ARTEMIS WAS RUNNING late to pick up Alexander at daycare. She hurried up the front walk and rang the bell.

"It's Mom!" Alexander's voice could be heard through the thick door.

Maddie opened it with a smile of greeting, her eyes tired, her baby sleeping in a sling on her chest. Artemis took all that in at a glance before Alexander crashed into her knees.

"Hello, my wonderful boy," Artemis cooed, bending to hug her son tightly. Then she straightened. To Maddie, she said, "Honey, you need a break. You're exhausted."

"Yes, well, Shayla doesn't like to sleep unless she's on me, so..." Maddie let the sentence hang in the air between them. She rubbed the baby's back through the sling and sighed heavily.

"So you do what you need to do," Artemis said knowingly. "But remember that if you get sick from lack of sleep, she will be the one who suffers."

Maddie gulped. "That wouldn't be good."

"Precisely. Have you tried a bassinet

attached to the side of the bed? There's a lip so that the baby can't roll toward you, and you'd be blocked by the bars on top and bottom," Artemis suggested. "But you'd still be right beside her, so she can feel your presence."

"That might work," Maddie said. "I'm willing to try anything at this point."

Artemis smiled and gave the other woman a hug, careful not to crush the baby. "You'll figure out what works for you, both of you, eventually." She stroked the baby's soft cheek with a gentle finger.

"What worked for you?"

"Oh, I just put him in a moonbeam and he was happy," Artemis said, adding with a wince, "Sorry."

Maddie rolled her eyes. "Goddesses."

Then she chuckled. "Well, it could be worse, right?"

Artemis nodded vehemently. "For sure. Good luck with Shayla. Come on, Alexander, we're going to Finley's for dinner."

"Lee?" Alexander grinned up at her. "I miss him. Why can't he live with us?"

"Good luck to you too!" Maddie said with a wink, closing the door behind them.

While Finley had become somewhat of a fixture at their house, he hadn't yet moved in. Artemis wasn't sure how to go about that conversation. After all, his brother Augustine hadn't moved in with his mate, Hera. Jaden was living with Maddie, but they had a newborn.

Is Finley waiting for me to extend the

invitation, or are we still in the "getting to know each other" phase of our relationship?

She felt a little silly thinking like that, since Finley had assured her that his bite marked her as his mate for life, but the truth was, they were only a few months into their relationship.

What happens if we move in together too soon and something I do bugs him?

Or the other way around?

"Mom?" Alexander asked, tugging on her hand.

"Yes, darling?" Artemis replied absentmindedly.

"I asked you a question, Mom," Alexander reminded her, pouting a bit.

Artemis bit her lip. "Sorry. I was thinking. Don't you think it's a little soon? We've only known Finley for a few months. If things were different, if you hadn't already known him, I wouldn't even have introduced the two of you yet."

"Why?" Alexander frowned. "I love him."

Is it really that simple?

"I do too, baby."

"I'm going to ask him." Alexander ran up the front walk of Finley's house.

Artemis blinked, startled because she hadn't realized they had already reached it. Then her brain caught up with what Alexander had said.

"Wait—"

But it was too late. Finley had opened the door, and Alexander was excitedly bouncing from one foot to the other, words falling all over each other as he tried to get everything out in one breath.

"I want you to live with us and Mom and I love you and wouldn't it be great to be all together as one family like Maddie and Jaden and Shayla but Mom thinks it might be too soon."

Maybe he didn't catch all that? Artemis hoped with a wince.

But Finley had looked up at her, his dark blue eyes piercing her soul, a tiny smile playing on his lips. "Why are you hiding at the gate?"

"I'm not," Artemis protested, joining them.

Finley drew her into a hug and pressed a light kiss to her lips, a promise of more to come. "You think it's too soon to move in together?"

"Maybe?"

"We've got our whole lives ahead of us. Why rush?"

Artemis cupped his chin in her hand. "I love you. You get me."

"I love you too."

Thank you for reading Artemis!

Turn the page to read about Witch's Delight, book one in my Blackthorn Academy Series.

One way or another, secrets will be exposed...

A student at Blackthorn Academy, Siobhan Doyle's goal is simple. She wants to focus on her studies, do the required time, and get out. She's eager to get on with this business of living and doesn't have time for anything else.

The instant she runs into Aiden Evans in the academy's mess hall, literally, Siobhan's world is turned upside down like the bowl of pudding upended on her head. As questions surface about her family's history, Siobhan is left seeking answers to the mysteries of the past. The old tombs in the basement of the school spill their secrets, mysterious tales of dark magic and murder, and lead her on a merry chase to find out the truth about her ancestors.

Will the tragedy she's discovered about her heritage shed a light on her future with Aiden, or will the truth tear her newfound mate from her before their relationship has barely begun?

Witch's Delight is book one in the Blackthorn Academy series, featuring an ambitious, curvy witch, and a hotter-than-sin, fire-breathing monster.

Snag your copy of Witch's Delight now!

If you enjoyed this book, please return to the retailer and leave a review. Your words mean so much and help us to continue writing the books you love.

Follow our Facebook page
Speed Dating with the Denizens of the Underworld Series

Watch your favorite online retailer for the other books in the Speed Dating with the Denizens of the Underworld series.

Watch for the other books in the
Speed Dating with the Denizens of the
Underworld Series

Lucifer

Samael

Hecate

Demi

Hell's Belle

Hades

Orion

Cassiel

Hera

Triton

Alastor

Athena

Zeus

Medusa

Spike

Artemis

ARTEMIS

Calliope

Mars

Pegasus

And More!

MORE FROM GINA

If you enjoyed this book, you may also enjoy…

Blackthorn Academy

Witch's Delight

Witch's Mystery

Witch's Pet

Witch's Baby

Speed Dating with the Denizens of the Underworld

Lucifer

Demi

Hera

Medusa

Artemis

FOLLOW GINA

Facebook
https://www.facebook.com/authorginakincade/

Newsletter Mailing List
https://landing.mailerlite.com/webforms/landing/r1r5n4

BookBub
https://www.bookbub.com/authors/gina-kincade

Blog/Webpage:
https://www.ginakincade.com/

Instagram
https://www.instagram.com/ginakincade/

Goodreads
https://www.goodreads.com/ginakincade

ABOUT GINA KINCADE

USA Today Bestselling Author Gina Kincade spends her days tapping away at a keyboard, through blood, sweat, and often many tears, crafting steamy paranormal romances filled with shifters and vampires, along with witchy urban fantasy tales in magical worlds she hopes her readers yearn to crawl into.

A busy mom of three, she loves healthy home cooking, gardening, warm beaches, fast cars, and horseback riding.

Ms. Kincade's life is full, time is never on her side, and she wouldn't change a moment of it!

Find more from Gina at:

https://www.ginakincade.com/

www.ingramcontent.com/pod-product-compliance
Lightning Source LLC
Chambersburg PA
CBHW061056210726
48294CB00001B/167